wild

WOMAN

Published 2022.
Printed in the United States of America.
ISBN: 979-8-9850420-2-3 (Paperback)
        979-8-9850420-0-9 (Hardcover)
        979-8-9850420-1-6 (EBook)

Library of Congress Control Number: 2021923519

To my Mom (Alison, "Shirley" & Great Mother)
a wise, wild woman
you are free now

"Within every woman there lives a powerful force, filled with good instincts, passionate creativity, and ageless knowing."

- Dr. Clarissa Pinkolla Estés, *Women Who Run With the Wolves: Myths and Stories of the Wild Woman Archetype*

wild WOMAN

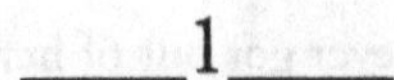

1

Once a week, I go to a meeting for women who have chosen crazies for husbands and are tired of hospital visits. Candy was one of us. She was a big woman, about 300 pounds, and her husband, she said, was only 165. He was a meth head, so she said he wasn't always that skinny. But he could beat her down with his fists and with his tongue. That's what we learned at those meetings, that words can hit, too. That stupid saying, "words can't ever hurt me," wasn't nothing but an awful lie. Seems like lots of things we were told as younguns turned out to be lies.

Once, during one of them, Candy's husband came barging in, his hair long and stringy under a sooted trucker's cap and his eyes wild and yellowed. He screamed at her, calling her a "fat-whore-good-for-nothin'." Candy's face looked as blank as drywall as she clutched her worn purse to her chest and rocked herself from her seat. One member, Willow, tried to hold Candy's hand to keep her from leaving; another muttered curse words under her breath. Candy didn't look back as she slowly made her way to the door where he was yanking on his belt buckle as if trying to hold his pants up while at the same time telling her what she'd be in for. But he didn't cross the threshold of the doorframe. He didn't dare step inside the room.

We could still hear him out in the hall, running his big mouth, long after the door had closed. Ten minutes of silence followed before we moved to holding hands to say the Lord's Prayer, which is how we ended our meetings.

Truth is, he might as well have been talking to all of us. Because you just don't know what a man in that state is capable of, once he gets you home.

Driving back to Mama's house that night on the outskirts of Eden's Gap, down the windy road to her house, scared me more than ever. Each turn, each pine tree that my car lights flashed upon, I just swore I was gonna see Jim standing there, shotgun barrel pointed right at my head.

Mama had some dinner saved for me. By then, she'd rarely say anything about my meetings. Most I ever got out of her was a useless "praise Jesus" comment, but then she'd have dinner warming for me in the oven which was her way of saying, "It's gonna be all right somehow."

A couple of months after I met Candy, after her husband dragged her out of that church basement, he killed her. Another tragedy. But you see, I'm betting she knew he would. Maybe she even welcomed it. That's the state we get to, loving a man who don't love you back and only thinking you've got one way out.

§

When I moved back in with Mama, I stopped smoking pot altogether though at times I thought I would die without a fix. My anxiety was running so high those days. But I didn't even try to sneak it like when I was in high school, she was being so kind to me.

Mama was religious, so she didn't even drink because that was a sin. I don't think she'd had a sip in her whole life. I'd thought she sure didn't know what she was missing. Jack 'n' Coke is a wonder drug when somebody's done knocked you upside the head with a frying pan or taken a belt buckle to your backside. I liked the sweet taste of Jack Daniels, and weed was all right by me, but luckily I never got much into pills.

My best friend, Angela, however, had prescriptions from four different pharmacies, all within a sixty-mile radius (and that there is in the country) before she got arrested. I didn't have the motivation it took to be a pill-head.

§

My older brother Danny was the first to get me high. We were at a barn party one October night, after the Bruins beat the Wildcats at home. I was in eighth grade then. Danny was a Miracle Junior, meaning it was a miracle he hadn't dropped out of school yet. But he and his loser buddies were out behind the barn passing around a joint. The air was sweet all around them, and when I walked up he handed it to me.

One thing I can say is that before I ran off and married Jim and before my brother got into the kinds of drugs that will steal your soul, we were close. Growing up the way we did, Daddy being long dead and no good besides, and Mama being all into God and her church, well, we had each other.

So when I joined him and his friends, he didn't say anything and they knew better than to wonder what I was doing there. Danny passed the joint to me. I put it up to my lips and breathed it all in, like I was blowing up one of those cheap party balloons but sucking in instead of out and coughed so hard I about threw up my dinner. Of course, they all laughed at me. "Fuck all y'all," I said before walking back towards the bonfire.

"Don't be mad, Charlie!" my brother called out to me.

At the fire, someone, a tall, lanky kid maybe a year older than me, handed me a cold beer. I drank and drank until he grabbed it out of my hands. It tasted like sour bread, but I liked it the same way folks like buttermilk. Then, with both the effect of the hit off that joint and the beer running into my belly, I started feeling all right—nothing too special. I burped, and then I felt my face ease up. I was grinning and damn...I got hungry. That was the first time I got high and hungry but it sure wasn't the last.

When I was living in the trailer behind the tire place, and wasn't trying to be a '50s homemaker to my useless husband, I smoked weed and ate. Now, I'm not real fat, but unlike my mama who's small-framed, I turned out more like my daddy, big-boned.

Of course my size never hurt me as far as getting the attention of some man, but I figured they were only after one thing. Maybe that's why Mama found religion. But then men don't care whether you got religion or not—my way of thinking was they'd fuck and beat you all the same.

My daddy beat the shit out of my mama when he was alive and Danny told me once that he'd seen Pawpaw backhand Granny, my daddy's mama, for asking him a question while he was watching football on the TV. Danny wasn't but seven. I was too young to remember, but Danny says that Granny walked in and asked Pawpaw what kind of chips he wanted with his sandwich. She must have blocked him from seeing some big play, and Danny said Pawpaw moved so fast in his recliner from sitting to standing, that he about knocked over his TV tray, a full ashtray, and newspapers, as the back of his hand smacked her square on the side of her face. "Goddammit, woman. Don't NEVER interrupt me watchin' no goddamn football again. I'd done told you…"

Then Danny said that Granny, stunned, said, "The children, Harley, don't you take the Lord's name in vain in front of the children," as she headed back into the kitchen with a visible red streak across her face.

Maybe my daddy learned it from his daddy. One thing I know is all Mama's praying and churchgoing didn't save her from Daddy's fists. If he hadn't died of a heart attack when I was eight, she may have met her God in Heaven sooner than he met his Devil in Hell.

§

Not all men are bad, so I've been told. Mostly once I started going to the meetings and heard the women talk about how they got out, recovered, and found men who respected them. I didn't understand why they kept coming to the meetings long after getting what they wanted all along. I was to learn, in time, that it was what lived in us we were recovering from.

Before my meeting days, I loved one man with all my heart, and that there was my brother Danny. Sadly, he'd up and left Mama and me. He got into the hard drugs and wasn't the same person I'd known when I was a girl. But I never stopped loving him for the man I knew him to be.

From as early as I can remember, I used to have the scariest nightmares. One nightmare was of these mean wolves. In it, I was sitting on the sofa in the living room, and all of a sudden, a pack of them came down the chimney. They snarled at me, and one lunged into my stomach. The darkest, biggest one tore at my flesh. I screamed out and woke up drenched in sweat. Danny was the one who was right there beside me, patting my head, telling me it'd be all right. "Just a bad dream, Charlie…I'm here," he'd say all gentle-like.

Even though he could also give me the most shit of anybody, I never doubted he'd put himself in front of a train for me.

§

I always wondered where he learned to be so sweet and how could this boy who loved me so run off and leave me. I missed him hard.

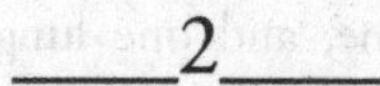

I was sixteen-and-a-half when I met Jim. Jim Randall Wilson, Jr. His daddy ran the tire shop next to the gas station off Highway 76. Jim was four years older than me, and when I saw him for the first time, I felt a desire in me that was as close to being possessed as I could imagine.

I'd ridden with Danny to get a patch on one of the tires on his Ford pickup. We pulled in and Danny parked us in front of the opened garage door, the other one pulled all the way down, a wall of black spray-painted glass panes and metal. To the left of the garage sat an old Pinto, hood open, next to a banged-up Chevy pickup, about the same year as Danny's Ford. A blue Ford Escort pulled up to one of the gas pumps, just as Jim walked out from the shadows of the garage in front of us.

He was fine. He had on a plaid shirt and a pair of tight Wranglers showing off the best ass my sixteen-year-old eyes had ever seen. He was tall, over six foot, and though he talked racing with my brother, he kept turning around to look at me.

"Yeah, that Earnhart is, man, he is...Damn."

Danny, in his muffled way replied, "Shit right. He whooped ass in Talladega Saturday."

"You know the tires they have on them cars? What I wouldn't give to drive one of them cars. Damn."

They pulled the truck into the garage, and I was left to wander around outside. The man driving the Escort walked by me to go inside the office to pay. The front window was layered in signs for Texaco, Gulf, Esso, Standard

Oil, Marlboro, Camel, Budweiser, Miller Genuine Draft, and Coors. There was a standard cab seat from a truck next to the office door, like a couch, with a metal ashtray stand beside it full of butts. I walked off to the side of the gravel lot that was the property, nearer to the tree line. There were Bud cans scattered about, a few smashed and rusting.

I smoked me a cigarette, wishing I had a cold Coke to drink, secretly checking my hair and lip gloss in my little compact mirror. I said a prayer of thanks that I'd thought to put makeup on that day. Most, I'm just too damn lazy, unlike my mama. She never goes out of the house without her face made. She'd say, "It ain't ladylike and no man's gonna even look at you without you tryin' to look pretty." I rarely paid her no mind because I thought she was old fashioned and didn't know what it was like to have attention from a boy I wanted.

I'd already been felt up and fingered by one boy, and I didn't see what the big deal to it all was. Felt like he was sticking a pencil up inside and digging it around. I sure couldn't see what he was getting out of it. But, Lord, if he didn't come all on my leg and out of breath say, "Look what you done." I didn't get so much as an itch from his bony finger. It was his attention that made me feel like something, like I'd gotten the only A in the class. I can't quite explain it, but I can say I'd never gotten an A my whole life.

Some girls my age had already had sex, and they acted all old. People called them sluts behind their backs, even the boys that had fucked them. I wasn't waiting to have sex, so much, because I wasn't believing there was somebody out there that special for me to wait for. I didn't want to disappoint Danny. He warned me about being slutty and said it would make him look bad with me being his little sister. "Besides," he'd say, "you ain't like that."

The reason I was wearing make up at all was because I'd gotten new teal mascara and had to wear it. Despite Mama's religious devotions and us not having so much, among the church ladies, appearances were up there with having the best rhubarb pie in the county. We stopped by Kmart regularly. She made sure I had all the primping supplies a girl my age could want. It was in that moment waiting for Jim to come back out and see me that I appreciated what Mama had been trying to get me to understand about men.

"Who's she? Your girl?" I heard Jim ask Danny as they walked out from the garage.

"What? Her?" Danny replied, pointing to me as I was pretending I had better thoughts to think than the likes of them. "Naw, man, Charlie's my little sister."

Danny went inside to pay while Jim backed the truck out right near where I was standing. As he got out, my heart started going into double time. "Hey," he said looking at me like he wanted to take a fresh bite.

"Hi," I mumbled, starting to feel the sweat under my arms and along my back.

"Danny's sister, huh?"

"Yep."

"Cool. You at Walterboro?"

I was dumb near silent. "Yeah."

"I graduated from there in '87. Played baseball."

"That's cool," I said managing to show teeth, hoping my mouth was in the shape of a smile.

"Yeah, love me some baseball. More than racing even."

"It's alright," I said, even though I'd never paid a lick of attention to anything but football and only because it was hard to get away from it where we were.

At that point, Danny came out. Jim turned his back to me and nodded at Danny, like he hadn't been talking to me. Danny got in the truck, as did I, and we left. In the side mirror, I could see Jim standing closer to the road, under the metal red and white sign for the tire place that said in bold, black letters: Randall Wilson Garage – Tires and Gasoline. He was watching us head up the highway.

"You like him?"

"Who?" I acted all stupid.

"Jim, you dumbass. I saw y'all talking."

"Don't know nothing 'bout him. Why? You like him? Y'all's doing a lot of talking yourself."

He shrugged me off and reached across the dash to get his pack of Marlboro Reds and his lighter and lit him a stogie. He tapped me on the arm, handing me one. I took it, taking a long inhale. I remember, like a long pause, turning to look at the trees going by. The sky was so blue and clean-looking, and the sun sparkled through the woods, like daytime fireflies. I rested my elbow on the rolled-down window feeling the cool air on my arm and side of my face, as thoughts of Jim started yanking on me.

I hated not knowing more about him. I wondered if he was with anybody and when I would see him again. I started feeling like any ease I had was being pulled out of my chest and an unsettling force was moving in. I took another long drag, trying to get ahold of myself.

§

It was no use. I wanted a reason to go back to the tire place. I rarely drove anywhere unless I was with Mama going with her to Claudia's to have her hair done, Ingles for groceries, or our Kmart trips. One morning, I came close to driving her car over a pile of nails, seeing if I could puncture a tire. I rummaged around the wooden shed at the back of the house, found a packet of two-inchers I thought would do the trick, when Danny yelled at me to stop my dilly-dallying.

"What the hell you doin' in Daddy's shed? Are those...nails?"

"Project for school," I said as I shoved them in my jean jacket pocket.

I felt like I could cut steel with my teeth, wanting to see Jim so badly and thinking it would never happen. Seeing him was becoming a need more than a want, out of my control, and it wasn't easing up on me.

I moved like a drum kit, slamming cabinets and doors and banging pots and pans, helping in the kitchen one night.

"Who pissed in your cornflakes?" my brother said.

"Daniel. Language!" Mama scolded him.

"Ain't nothin,'" I growled back at him.

Then to me, she said, "Charlene Louise, do you have to stomp around so?" She probably thought I was about to have my period, which she'd never mention, because she never did ask what was wrong.

§

Then one day after school, Danny drove up as I was sitting on the front steps smoking a cigarette. Mama was at Wednesday night Bible study and would be gone until late, so I could sit there, not worrying about her catching me. He ran up the stairs past me shouting, "Hey, there's a party tonight up Mill Mountain Road. You've been a complete bitch for the last week, but you can come if you want."

"Sure. Why not?" I yelled at him, already in the house, though I was so relieved to have something to do besides feel like I was going to lose my ever-living mind. School didn't distract me, and Angela was getting about as fed up with me as my brother.

"Lord, Charlie," she'd said last time we talked, "you talk about Jim like you'd give him half a kidney. You only met the guy once."

"I know, Ang, I know. But you didn't see him. He didn't talk to you like he talked to me."

"I've heard some stories…" she'd added.

"Never mind. Forget it," I'd said, and I meant it.

Danny came out of the house wearing a different shirt. "Gotta get beer and some smokes. Back in thirty." He patted the top of my head as he skipped down the stairs past me. I pulled away as if annoyed. He hopped in his truck and headed down the drive.

I stared after him a long while, in a daze that lingered behind my brother. It was starting to get dark and chilly. The leaves were turning orange and red and dancing from the tip of their stems. I sat there thinking about how since the tire shop I'd gone to bed every night with different fantasies about Jim running through my head. In one, I was walking down the aisle of Mama's church, with its red carpet matching the red cushions on the pews. I had my hand around my brother's arm as he led me toward the preacher and Jim, who I imagined to be looking at me as if he'd never seen anything prettier in all his life.

I sat on the steps, getting colder yet unable to move, stuck in my other fantasy about me pulling up to the tire shop in Mama's blue Mercury Sable with a flat, barely making it to the garage part, when Jim would come running out and say, "Baby, what's the matter?" He'd open my door and as I stepped out, he'd put his arms around me. I would imagine being able to smell his cologne, musky and manly, as I'd put my head on his chest and he'd kiss my cheek. Then he'd say, "We're gonna get you all fixed up. Don't worry your pretty little head about a thing."

I had come up with a million of those dreams of him and me. I knew what our house looked like, with light blue shutters and a white porch swing, a blue floral cushion with matching pillows. I knew that our bedroom had a poster bed and two dressers that came as a set. On my dresser I'd see all our pictures: our prom, our wedding, and pictures of our kids, two boys and two girls.

I got lost in thoughts of my yellow kitchen with tiles of flying geese on them. I would see myself frying chicken in a large iron skillet, just in time for Jim getting home from a hard day's work. I'd imagine hearing his truck pull into the drive as the kids ran down the hallway yelling, "Daddy's home! Mama! Daddy's home!"

My imagination was as strong as my desire was for Jim. I didn't know a thing about raising a family or, less simply, love. With that thought, I dropped my head between my knees, letting my hair fall over my face. I knew I'd better hurry up and get ready, knowing Danny wasn't going to wait for my ass and knowing I would die if he went to the party without me.

§

It was almost time for Mama to get home before Danny finally showed back up. I'd been too anxious to eat anything. I'd smoked half a pack already and my fingers and toes were numb from the cold, October mountain air. "It's about damn time!" I shouted at him, though he couldn't hear me over the sound of his truck engine. I hopped in beside him. "Jesus, Danny, I'm fucking freezing," I said, hoping to make him feel bad for taking so long.

Backing up to turn around, way too quickly, he replied, "I can't help it that you're a giant dumbass, sitting in the goddamn cold, now can I?" I didn't say nothing else to him the whole way.

I could tell he was already messed up on booze and whatever else he'd really gone to the "store" for and that he'd probably leave me as soon as we got to the party. I reached into the case of Budweiser on the seat between us and pulled me out a beer. After the first three swallows, I warmed up.

Danny drove us along the gravel and potted Mill Mountain Road the three miles to the top where there was an opening and where an old Methodist chapel sat. Finally I asked him, "How'd you find out about this anyway?"

"Why's it matter?"

"It don't. Just trying to make conversation."

"Jim Wilson. When I's getting gas the other day, said he and some of his buddies were having a party. Said I should bring some girls." My heart froze hearing Danny say Jim Wilson's name and that he was going to be at the party. All of a sudden, my face felt hot, and I needed that cold air again.

"Oh," I said. "That guy from the tire place?"

"Yeah, yeah. Him. I already done said. Your hearing busted or something?" We wound our way closer to where there would be an open area of dirt and grass, where we could park.

I never knew why the cops never broke up the parties that went on up there. Most of us were underage. I also never knew how nobody ever died driving home afterwards. There was no other way down but the single track of road, and one side of it was a straight drop to the trees below.

By the time we pulled up, there was already maybe twenty trucks and cars there. I used the rearview mirror to put on more lipstick and check my bangs. Why I would have thought that they would have moved is beyond me, since they were Aquanetted, Ultrahold-style.

"You better put that mirror back right like it was," Danny huffed. I made a face at him he didn't see. "Come on." I think he was looking for somebody himself. He grabbed the case, handing me one, and got out, slamming his door without saying "Goodbye" or "Have a great time." He just left me to wander the party by myself. I could hear "Sweet Child O' Mine" blasting from a nearby truck.

In the distance, I made out a line of white pine and chestnuts that looped around the small stone chapel built way before any of us, our grandparents included, were born. Twenty or thirty feet to the left of it, I made out a group of guys standing next to a campfire. I popped open the beer, took a few swallows and headed in that direction.

"Gotta stogie?" I asked a short, stocky guy wearing a green John Deere hat and thick black and blue flannel shirt. He handed me a Camel unfiltered and offered me a light. That's when I saw Jim walking over to us and whipped my head so fast looking away I nearly gave myself a cricked neck. That faint, wispy feeling I'd associated with weak girls pushed in the back of my knees.

"Hey!" he shouted, not to me. The boys had been passing around a whiskey bottle and liter of Coke. Jim took the whiskey and downed about a half-a-minute swallow of the stuff. Then he was standing next to me.

"Your turn," he said while handing me the bottle. I took a sip and looked up at him in front of me, so tall and goddamned good-looking as his eyes reflected the partially-eaten-pie shape of the moon. "Aren't you Danny's little sister?" I could smell the whiskey and smoke on his breath.

My eyes watered a bit from the burn of the Beam, and I reached for some Coke to ease my throat. A slight grin slid over his face as he stood there, not handing it to me. Looking back, I wonder if that was a sign, or a red flag, as the women's group would call it. Maybe I should have walked away right then. But I didn't know anything about warning flags, and the pull from him on me was as strong as the pull that had my feet anchored to the soft, damp grass below me. I couldn't have turned away from that man if I had wanted to.

I tried again to take the bottle from him, but he reached out quick and grabbed my wrist tight. "What? You can't handle it?" he teased, before letting out a deep, husky laugh and handing me the liter bottle, granting me sweet relief. I chugged down as much as I could, though the burn had made its way down to my stomach. I stayed strong, held my chin up.

He turned from me, like he had at the tire place when my brother came out and saw us. He started talking to another girl who had walked up. She was half my size, with long, dark hair and her jeans tucked into her boots. She oozed lust from her hips' sway, like the dribble of juice down the side of the apple. I didn't know, know her, but I knew her like every woman knows another woman, and I didn't like her any more than I liked accidentally stepping in a cow patty.

That's when the short stocky guy came back over to stand next to me. "So...Charlie, you said it was? I seen you around at school..." I couldn't listen. All I wanted was to get ahold of more beer to wash down the sudden panic wringing tight my chest, Jim's attention stolen by that Jezebel. Instead, I blurted out, "I gotta pee," louder than I meant to and walked off to the woods.

My head was buzzing. I was nauseous but less from what I'd drunk. I stumbled around to the other side of the chapel, the stone catching and tossing glints of moonlight, away from most of the people. As I made my way two rows back into the woods, I ran into a couple of girls who were already "making tinkle," as my Granny used to say. "This here's a good spot," one of the girls hollered out. I ducked behind a young white oak and undid my jeans.

I could hear and see a semi-shadowed girl say to her friend, "That's Danny's little sister." I didn't have as much privacy as I'd hoped.

"Your brother's cute," her friend agreed. I had been hearing that most of my life; the girls loved my brother. They giggled away, drunk as I was, leaving me to wobble-pee in peace.

Surprisingly, I had managed to not pee on or in my shoes, and as I looked up, I saw a body, in the distance yet getting closer. When it got right too close, I could see it was a he and that it was Jim. I yanked up my panties and jeans as one, nearly giving myself a wedgy.

"There you are," he said, controlling his slur.

"Had to pee," I said, as if I might have been hanging out by myself in the woods looking for gnome people or something.

"No shit," he spit back. He walked right up and put his hands on my waist. "Charlie, Charlie, Charlie," he said.

Every moment of my daydreams felt like it was happening with his hands on me. He pulled my hips to him and leaned into me. With one hand, and I remember it clearly because it was a moment I tried over and over to recreate later, he took my chin and lifted my face and lips to his. He kissed me. His tongue moved into my mouth and the wetness our tongues danced around each other. He got hard against me and his breathing was as deep and as desperate as I had been feeling for him over the last, long week.

"You turn me on," he said as he reached up under my shirt and bra, recklessly running his cold, calloused hand across my chest. He kissed my neck, and I was as wet between my legs as if I had peed my pants after all.

My fantasies were cut short by someone's laughter echoing nearby, making me hesitate. Yards off, a few drunk folks stumbled around the corner, like the ground was giving way. "What?" he said, smiling. "You shy?" At that, he let go of me. "Gotta take a piss."

Jim walked ten feet off and turned his back to me. I didn't know what to do. I was paralyzed. I was scared thinking I'd lost him, the moment over, my dream over, while at the same time scared at the thought of being a fool waiting for him to finish pissing. The wobbly kids never made it our way.

"Where did you think you were going?" Jim called out, even though no part of my body had moved since he'd stepped away. He barreled up behind me reaching again for my waist. "I wasn't done with you." He turned me around as we were before. I thought there would never be anything that could make me that happy. Jim kissed me quick and hard before taking my hand and leading me out of the woods back toward the party. Back in my dream, dreaming on, I was flying.

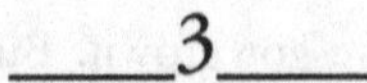

3

Weeks had passed, and I was in the kitchen helping Mama finish the last of the dishes when she started in on me seeing Jim. "What's so special about that boy? His family don't go to church. His mama don't even leave their house."

Rolling my eyes, I said, "Not everybody has to go to church. Don't mean nothin.'" She looked at me as if the Devil was standing behind me looking at her over my shoulder.

I had been having Danny take me down to the tire place nearly every day after school. Since Jim worked, I figured it was the right thing to do— support my man. Since I didn't participate in after school activities or have my own job, I was like a stray animal waiting for scraps of Jim's attention.

He wasn't affectionate in the way I'd daydreamed, but I knew he liked me being there. Once, after a customer left, he brought me out a cold Coke and sat with me to have a smoke break. Another time, when a customer was still there, he was talking to them but looking over at me, like he couldn't wait to put me up against the back of the shop once they'd gone. That made me excited in a way I could never explain to Mama.

"Don't you talk like that in this house!" she snapped back at me. "It's bad enough my own children don't go to Sunday church with their widowed mama. Bad enough when everybody asks where my children are."

"Just tell them nosey church folks to mind their own business," I shot back. "I don't know why you care so much what people think of you, Mama. You're a good person. That's all that should matter."

"Good Christians tend church regular, and I won't stop praying my kids will honor their Lord, Jesus Christ, as they should by going to his house on Sunday with their dear mama," she said, in her way letting me know I wouldn't be winning an argument about God and church with her. Facts were facts, she was telling me.

I knew what her church meant to her and how hurt she was that Danny and I stopped going when we got grown. But I didn't like how they all talked about each other. Plus, mine and Danny's business wasn't the worst of what some of their kids were up to. At least not then.

She handed me a dish to dry. "I don't know about a boy who don't come by to meet the mama of the girl he loves," she said, "It ain't right." I stopped still, just staring at the plate in my hand. Her saying that stung. I wanted to smash the dish on the counter, storm out and smoke a joint. Instead, I went on to dry it, and she handed me another.

Mama moved on to talking about Millie, a woman from her church who was married to Bobby Jenkins, a trucking man. Bobby kept his big rig parked along Highway 76, a mountain road full of switchbacks and not wide enough for coming head-to-head with an 18-wheeler, when he wasn't out on one of his cross-country hauls. Bobby and Millie had been married since she was sixteen and despite the fact that he was a decent man, at least as far as we knew, Millie had her own set of problems—four of them, to be exact. They had two girls and two boys and all four of them as riddled with craziness as a person could be. Of course, Mama never said it that way. She only talked about how Millie cried almost every Sunday, when you just didn't do that kind of thing in public, not even in church.

I was half-listening, as I was stirred up about what she'd said about Jim and him not loving me. I kept thinking about how Mama was no expert on love, I could tell her that. I wrung out the dish towel, now wet and heavy, and she went on. "She sobs the whole sermon, Charlene. Through the whole thing, bless her heart. Her youngest boy is meaner than the Devil. Bless his heart, that boy is."

Now, I knew that my mama thought Millie was to blame for her children's shortcomings, because she thought the root of all suffering was that you'd made God mad. That's the other reason why Danny and me not attending worried her so.

Unlike her, I was mad at God. I thought there was no way he cared about us no matter what we'd do. He gave us a mean daddy and then let him die. It didn't matter how much Mama prayed and did her church service, my feelings were that God somehow still thought she and her children should suffer.

§

Mama and I went on and on like that about God and Jim until I moved out of her house six months after Easter, 1992. I had dropped out of high school and married Jim, but not in her church, which couldn't have been more shameful to her. Jim had said plainly to me, "I ain't setting foot in no church. God never done nothing good for me. Shit, what'd God or church ever do for you?"

Since he was going to be my husband, and I felt about the same, it seemed right to oblige him rather than Mama. When I told her what we weren't going to do, she came near to swearing at me. And since she doesn't swear, she stopped talking to me altogether.

I didn't have much to take with me to my new home, which turned out not to be the house of my countless daydreams, the one with the Robin's-egg-blue shutters and matching porch swing. Jim hoisted my suitcase into the back of his truck, barely waiting for me to get in the other side before peeling out, probably as another huff at a nonexistent God and at my mama.

We screeched to a halt in front of my new house, which was an old trailer on the property behind the tire place. It was a single-wide on a clear-cut patch of pine, now dirt, and had been whiter at one time, maybe, with a brown-gold trim. The foundation wasn't but stacked cinder blocks. Lattice had been cut to line the bottom, like a bed skirt, but only one half of the trailer had been wrapped. The rest of the wood was stacked against the side, warping from rain and sun.

Jim's parents owned it, and we stayed there rent free. But nothing is free, another tidbit that didn't take me long to learn.

His mama, Mrs. Bernice Wilson, never came by. She was an extra-large woman with only hate in her eyes. She rarely left her house only a quarter mile up the dirt road behind us on the same property, so I met her less than a handful of times. Jim's daddy, however, came by regularly. I made both he and Jim lunch most days, but he'd stop in whether Jim was with him or not. I'd hear the metal screen door slam and his footsteps to the fridge. Then I'd hear the popping of the top of his beer can, hollering for me: "Girl!" If I didn't come out fast enough, he'd come looking.

The first time, I thought he'd made an honest mistake, since my t-shirt was still wrapped around my head, me working my arms in it as fast as I could. He didn't turn away, just stayed too long staring all dirty at my chest. "I ain't dressed!" I yelled.

"Nice tits," he murmured as he headed back to plop himself down in Jim's La-Z-Boy recliner and flip the channel to NASCAR. When I realized he wasn't sorry, the anger welled up in the back of my throat and then sunk back to a charred pit in my gut.

I walked by to the kitchen with him parked in front of the TV, having already forgotten me. I asked him if he wanted some macaroni and cheese, like I'd forgotten, too.

§

Mr. Wilson's attempts to see me half-dressed, or talk to me through the bathroom door when I was on the toilet, or the one time when I reached over him to put his beer on the TV tray and he grabbed my "nice tit," started happening more and more.

One day Jim came home early enough to catch his daddy's paws on me. Mr. Wilson moved his hand so fast you'd have thought a sniper shot it off. Jim didn't say anything to his daddy; he acted like he hadn't seen it.

Jim walked past both of us to the back to change his shirt before leaving shortly after Mr. Wilson excused himself and left to head up to his own house. Jim didn't say a word to me, the door slamming behind him. I knew where he had gone off to and knew it'd be late before he came back.

I sat for hours in the same spot his daddy had been, but instead of staring at the TV, I was staring at that rusted metal door, wishing and wanting him to come home, my breathing thin, like I'd run out of oxygen any minute.

I knew he was out at Tank's, a nasty trucker bar with a big rebel flag and rotted-out wooden slats for windows. As bad as Tank's was, there were also women that hung around, like drunken horseflies, relentless and painful. It liked to have killed me waiting for him, and yet I couldn't have moved if a host of angels had tried to drag me off that chair.

When Jim's truck engine cut off hours later, I blinked rapidly, focusing my eyes on where he would soon be—the front door. Sure enough, there he was, standing tall above me. I smiled. His hand swung down, landing across my cheek with a loud smack. I sat there, seeing stars on the cheap wood-paneled wall.

"You dirty fucking whore!" he spat, his words slurred by the booze I could smell on his breath. The relief I felt when he pulled into the yard hid quick like a scared child. I started trembling. "What, you fucking bitch? What? You think I don't see things? You think I don't see what a whore you are when I ain't around?"

I knew better than to try and answer him, console or convince him otherwise. I knew better, like knowing what color my eyes were. I knew better. His hand swung at me again. The back of his knuckles caught my temple and my jaw shook. I felt blood in my mouth.

"I don't never wanna see you and my daddy...you...you disgusting...." With that, he turned and headed to our bedroom.

I took my time getting up. I used the walls to steady myself as I made my way to the bathroom. I washed my face and saw the bruise forming on my cheek.

I looked in on Jim, face down in our bedroom, passed out drunk. I took off my sweatpants and crawled in bed beside him, wishing he'd put his hand around me and tell me he was sorry.

Jim never said he was sorry. And he never could stand up to Jimmy Senior, despite being so much taller than his daddy. So that left him to take it out on me. I didn't understand it, so I made it okay inside my head as best I could.

§

Aside from running errands for Jim's mama—she drank more milk than a single cow made in a month—there wasn't a whole lot I had to occupy myself with, stuck up in our sad-excuse-for-a-house trailer behind the shop. I could have been working if Jim didn't think it insulted his manhood somehow. Of course he'd never admit it. Instead, he'd say, "Good-for-nothing at home is good-for-nothing at some job."

I passed the time watching lots of TV. I never got into soap operas, like the Young and the Restless or Days of Our Lives. For one, I thought they were stupid, as if they'd ever get to the point and be done with it. And two, they were interrupted every five minutes with dumb Mr. Clean commercials.

Instead, I got into old movies on the American Movie Classics channel where men were gentlemen and women were treasures. Or there were the stories where people were poor and struggled, like "How Green Was My Valley," but they wanted someone in the family to live a better life than them and that someone would!

All my olden-days movie watching got me into trouble, because for some reason I got the idea one day that I would make homemade biscuits for Jim. I figured every true Southern woman needed to know how to make a buttermilk biscuit from scratch, so that's what I figured I'd start with. I wanted to call Mama and ask her about the recipe, but since she'd stopped talking to me for marrying Jim, I made one up.

I didn't have a whole lot of baking supplies or counter space to work with in that fabricated space called our kitchen. I made do with a TV tray for dumping the flour and rolling out the dough. AMC was on in the living room showing the story of a classy, uptown New York City fellow whose sweetheart was engaged to an older, and more powerful man—a love triangle. As I pulled the sticky dough from the rolling pin, I got lost in an idea of a life so completely far off from my own, it might as well have been about someone from China.

I got to thinking I would be a beautiful and dainty but meaningful housewife. When my man would come home from a hard day's work, I would have the table all set, a fresh-baked cherry pie cooling on the counter, fried chicken and greens warming in the oven.

Just as I would have touched up my lipstick and reddened my cheeks with rouge, spraying myself with perfume from a fancy glass bottle with a gold pump and tassel, I would hear him pull into the driveway. When he'd walk in the front door, I'd be standing there all made up, ready to greet him. "Hi, honey. So glad you're home," I'd say in a sexy but pure voice, our children within earshot.

In my fantasy, that's when he'd pull me to his chest in a strong-armed manly way, my neck tilted back as I looked up to him. My prince. My knight. My sophisticated man, capable of providing the right kind of security for our family and the right kind of affection for me as he would tell me I was the prettiest thing in all of the Eastern seaboard and that he was the luckiest man ever, because I was his wife and he'd take care of me every live long day.

And then he would lean in and kiss me. Not in the open mouthed, spit-filled groping tongue way, but lips pressed to lips—strong and passionate and gentle as if all he'd said was true.

Anyway, my fantasies tricked me into trying my hand at making biscuits. But unlike the movies, my good intention wound me up in the hospital. My biscuits came out like sun-scorched dirt.

Jim came home all right. He stomped his heavy-footed way into the trailer, and without a single thought of me, headed back to the bedroom to change his shirt.

"Hey, Jim," I called to him from the kitchen. I had just pulled the biscuits out of the oven, and they were cooling on the stove. I proceeded to get out some honey and butter. He didn't answer.

"Jim!" I shouted, louder that time. Again he didn't respond, so I walked back to the bedroom and pulled back the sheet that was our door, to see him shuffling through a pile of clothes on the floor near the bed.

"These clean?" he demanded.

"Yeah. You know I do laundry every Wednesday." I was aching for him. "I made biscuits," I said, hardly a whisper.

"Speak up," he huffed.

"I said, 'I made biscuits,'" getting the words out a little louder. "From scratch," I managed to add, letting loose a crack of hope. He turned around and dead-panned looked at me as if I was a fly he was zeroing in on before swatting. I instinctively stepped back a foot into the hallway. "I just thought you might want..."

"What? You don't cook." He almost laughed, but didn't care enough to do so.

"I want you to try one."

"You do, huh?" He half-said as he picked out a blue plaid wrangler shirt and went to remove his grimy work shirt that he slung over to me.

"Well, yeah. I do." I said so carefully, so desperate for him to pay attention to me, but knowing from time and time again how to hold back

24

emotion, for even happy ones could set him off. Funny, too, how over the years Jim began calling me dumb and boring. Said I was cold. More like I just fell farther and farther inside myself, where no sunlight dared to show.

Years later, I learned that you can't keep the sunlight out, because it shines from within. For a long time I didn't know that, and I thought Jim Wilson Jr. was my only way of feeling the warm rays of the sun.

Looking down at Jim's work shirt in my arms and seeing him snap up his clean one, it dawned on me that he was heading out. A hole began opening up in me, like a dark funnel with a force stronger than a rip-roaring, Oklahoma summer sky tornado that was going to suck me into it. This funnel wasn't going up, either; it only went down. Way down. "Please, try a biscuit, Jim. Before you go out. Again."

He pushed past me to the bathroom. "Not hungry," he said as he shut the hollow wood door behind him. I could hear him unzip his pants and the sound of his piss hitting the toilet bowl. "What do you mean by 'again'?" he shouted at me as I heard him spray on his deodorant. "What the fuck you trying to say?" he said opening the door.

He stopped half an inch from me, his face in mine. I could smell the pine scent of his armpits along with his cigarette/Listerine breath as he snarled, "What the fuck does that mean? I said." Scared to move or say anything, I stood there not wanting him to move either. If only he'd take me in his arms and hold me. He snorted and moved to the kitchen. I followed him.

"I got butter and honey for them," I offered, as if the man had changed his mind. He opened the fridge, cracked open a Pabst Blue Ribbon, took a few swallows and looked past me. "I said I ain't hungry. Since when you get a hearing problem?"

He finished off the beer, then to my surprise, picked up a biscuit. "Here, let me get you a plate," I said like a fool. At that he knocked it against the metal sink. "Why'd I wanna eat this?" He threw it across the room towards the door. It rattled the metal screen. Not a crumb broke off. Blood drained from my head and my hands went numb. It was rare for me to react to Jim denying me in a way he'd ever see, but the funnel was yanking at my innards and howling in my ears. I knew he was heading out to some trash bar and would be with some trash woman and not me. And I had done the best I could by making biscuits, just like in those movies and in my fantasies.

As if in a blackout, I picked up a biscuit and hurled it at Jim with all the disappointment that was pulling me into the drain that was my life. By the time the shock on his face from the first one had worn off, he punched me in the mouth so hard that blood started flowing back into my head like a rushing, hot river.

I knew then that the immediate swelling of my face from the impact of his fist was as close to his arm cradling my back as I was going to get. So, I picked up another biscuit to throw, and received another crash from his fist. My right eye started filling with blood, and a sharp pain cut through my temple.

After the fourth biscuit I threw, and the fourth punch I got back, Jim got tired of holding me that way. He shoved me back against the wall and picked up the tray, slinging the remaining six across the six square foot kitchen and began hitting me over the head with it until I was cradled on the burnt-orange linoleum. Over and over he hit me until he got bored, and I started losing consciousness. Finally, he dropped the tray and I faintly heard him walk out. "Goddamn bitch wife," was all I heard before passing out cold.

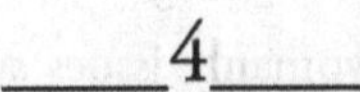

4

I woke up in the hospital. I recognized one of the nurses from the squinty corner of my good eye—left one this time. She must have sensed my coming to, because even though her back was turned, she said, "Hi there. How're you feeling?"

She was the sensitive one. Nurse Donna. For my times in the hospital, five in about three years, I got to know the staff so-so well and them me. Not all of the nurses gave a crap, like Nurse Shannon who was just a rotten bitch, mean as shit, where I felt like her having to come check on me was right out bothersome. Don't know why she'd ever become a nurse for hating people so much.

Nurse Donna seemed to care and was super gentle. She walked over to me and stuck a thermometer in my mouth, took my wrist in her tiny, soft fingers while looking down at me with her deep, brown old-lady eyes as she checked my vitals for the fiftieth time. I closed my good eye, my right one stuck shut so that even if Jesus stood before me, I wouldn't have been able to pry it open to get a glimpse of my mama's main man. My head was killing me and the sliver of light I had let in to see Nurse Donna only made the throbbing worse. "Now, now. Just rest, you hear? You've had a rough day," she said tenderly, laying my wrist back down on the bed beside me.

Straightening out the blanket around my shoulders as if tending to an infant, she asked me, "You warm enough, hon?" I managed to signal that I was because she took the thermometer out, scribbled some notes on my chart and walked out of the room after telling me that Dr. Willoughby would be in to see me soon.

The doctor's name was new to me, for normally in my visits I was assigned Dr. Floyd who'd been my doctor since I was a baby. I guess they do hospital rounds or whatever. I was always embarrassed around Dr. Floyd. He was old now, and he went to the big, fancy Presbyterian church in town. He seemed ashamed to be examining a young woman, especially when having to inform us about womanly issues such as menstrual cycles and regular breast exams.

When I got my first period, my mama, who disliked doctors or "modern-day hoohah" as she called it, took me to Dr. Floyd hoping he'd explain, in strict biological terms of course, the nature of a woman's body. She could cover the lust and sin part just fine by taking me and my brother Danny to church or by reciting Bible verses, but she wasn't about to talk about how it all worked. She left that to Dr. Floyd. To my relief, all he did that day was to walk in, hand me some pamphlets with pictures of my woman parts and some words I'd never heard of, like Fallopian tube and uterus, along with a box of generic pads saying the nurse would be in if I had any questions. The nurse was the one who told me about regular breast exams which seemed to me to completely defy anything the church said about touching oneself, but since I was mortified to be there in the first place, I didn't ask the question I most wanted to ask: Why did I have to bleed out of my monkey once a month? My best friend, Angela, later explained what Mama, God, and Dr. Floyd wouldn't.

It wasn't much different when Dr. Floyd would check on me at the hospital after Jim had beat me up the other four times. I'd hear him whispering outside the door with the nurses before walking in with my chart. Seemed to examine it as if he was grading some test I'd failed before turning around and walking right back out.

After Nurse Donna left, the room was dark, and I had no idea what time it was or how I'd even gotten to the hospital from my kitchen floor. I drifted off to sleep and must have been dreaming but still don't know for sure. I sensed a light growing far off as if down a long hallway. The light seemed to grow and get closer. I opened my eyes to see my hospital room lit up from something other than the bright overhead lights. It was a soft light, and my head had stopped hurting. I could see a rocking chair in the corner of the room and a small figure sitting in it. I wasn't afraid; I felt calm as a soft breeze in my chest. The million thoughts that normally ran through my head had stopped running.

"Charlie," the figure from the chair called out. I began to make out the figure of an old gray woman sitting in a rocking chair. I could see she was knitting what seemed to be a scarf with no end. "What's that?" I asked her, completely unafraid.

"A healing shawl," she replied, not even looking up. Her hands and fingers were moving rhythmically pulling and looping a light blue yarn in and out, over and under. I heard the click, click of the needles matching the beat in motion with her rocking and my breathing. My head felt heavy and I drifted into another kind of sleep—one that took me wandering deep into a forest. Then suddenly, I was struck with a powerful hunger, the worst I ever felt in my life. My stomach growled so loudly, it almost echoed off the mountainside I found myself stumbling along.

It was becoming dusk and the tall trees around me became stretched out, gangly arms against the gray-pink sky. I was finding it difficult to walk. I looked at my feet and saw that I was not wearing any shoes nor pants. Twigs under me snapped and cut my ankles and heels under my weight. Fear wrapped around my shoulders like a wet, wool blanket and I realized how alone I was in the dark woods. I was shivering and moving forward and could see my breath in the cold, damp air.

I was just skin and bones and feeling weak. Each step forward felt like the hardest thing I'd ever done. I started to cry. In the blur from my tears I fell over a large rock. How had I not seen that? My knee was bleeding, and I could see bone. Dear God, I was gonna die. As I lay there on the ground, my face nestled in a pile of leaves, I saw a light just above me. It looked to be a break in the side of the rock. I got up, using every bit of strength in my skinny arms to lift my head and sit me up. I rolled over on all fours and crawled up the ledge to the opening.

There I saw the strangest thing. Inside was a fire, and it was red and yellow, with billow clouds of blue and purple. The sparks from the wood crackled blue and purple, too. I crawled closer, completely taken by this fire of strange color. I almost didn't notice that along the back wall of the cavern, which looked to go back deep within the mountain, squatted the hairiest woman I'd ever seen.

In the mountains near where I was reared, I'd heard stories of inbreds. This one here was different. Despite her being so far back, I could hear her breathing like wind pouring through an open window, and I caught a glimpse of her soft, blue eyes which reminded me of my dear mama. Besides this being the strangest situation I'd ever found myself in, it not making a lick of sense to me, I heard a low growl rise from the back of her throat.

I'd have been more scared if I wasn't completely exhausted. I could no longer hold myself up and fell as a pile of bones to what was now just feet from this animal-woman creature. She began to sing and bay a melody known only to wolves, but shared so tenderly with me. My heart began to swell as her singing rose louder and louder until I felt her breathing and singing inside of me.

Though my eyes were shut tight, I sensed the blues and purples of the crackling fire rise in swirling circles of light around my ears and enter into my nose and mouth. I yawned wide and full. Her voice rumbled and shook the cavern, echoing down the long, hard rock as if she had worked to meld millions of years of solidified structure.

My bones rattled and danced beneath me, and I felt wild with an energy so intense that I couldn't stop it from picking me up. I let out the craziest, most maniacal of laughs. Like a hyena, I laughed and laughed. Tears flowed down my swollen cheeks, which were glowing from the light of the fire. I jumped and stomped my feet, all the while laughing. All the while the wild wolf woman sang and sang. Suddenly, she turned and looked out to the forest, the dark night with only a sliver of the moon's light providing sight. From the top of her voice and from deep within her gut, she yelled, "Git! You! Git!"

She started shooing me out into the night from which I'd come. I didn't hesitate. I took off as fast as I could go, running through the trees, the wind blowing my hair back, eyes keen to every root, stone, and broken branch before me.

I woke up realizing I must have been dreaming, but thinking I must be high on whatever pain pills they'd given me. I started coming to and had a strong sense that I was going have to get away from Jim for good—that maybe I could.

§

Dr. Willoughby had given me the okay to be released but said I couldn't drive. I called Mama. It was the first time I'd talked to her in years. "Hello?"

"Mama," I said, my voice sounding scraggly like an old man.

"Who's this?" she said, the faucet running water in the background behind her voice which sounded distant.

"Mama. It's me. Charlie."

"Charlene Louise?"

"Yes, Mama."

"Well, now. How's things?" she asked as if we talked every week.

"Can you come get me?" My voice was weak and my head throbbed just behind my right eye.

"Where you at, Charlene?" she asked.

"At the hospital. Things ain't so good now. Can you come get me?"

Not but an hour later, she looked small and frail coming into my room, a bag of clean clothes in her right hand while her left held onto the handle of her simple, navy leather purse. From what I could see, her Walnut brown hair was perfectly styled with round curls, teased just so, as if she'd left Claudia's moments before. Her hair wouldn't change shape for an entire week. Her coral lipstick lined her pursed lips and her eyes, well, as usual they sparkled blue like water dancing off of the ocean. Her face was powdery white like the old-timey kings and queens, and her eyebrows were freshly drawn. She looked out of place in my plain hospital room.

She disapprovingly took a look over the new bruises on my jaw and swollen eye. "Here ya go. Brought a change of clothes." Nurse Donna wasn't on when I was ready to head out, but she'd left me a note on the table beside my bed. It had a name and phone number on it. I took the bag from Mama and went into the little bathroom to change, tucking the note into one of the pockets of the old skirt that must have come from donations given to the church. Sometimes she'd have a trunk full of used clothes, towels, blankets, and the occasional mixer or other small kitchen appliances, as she was unashamed to ask anyone to give to the church and, in Jesus's name, to the poor.

Every movement I made hurt. It was as if every muscle and limb had taken the same beating as my face. My heart ached even worse as I fumbled with the clothes, the shirt being a button-up flannel of my brother's. I looked like one of those weird Wesleyan girls who aren't allowed to wear pants, with my plaid shirt on top and old lady skirt on bottom—two halves of the same body that look to disagree with one another.

Mama was on a mission to get us out of there without anyone seeing us because of the trouble I'd been in and because of how easy word got out. I didn't guess she considered that my face was like a billboard on a highway, giving away our shameful family secret.

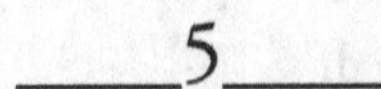

5

Mama got us home and got me settled into my old room. I had gotten Vicodin to take with me for the pain and was out of it. I let her bring me some of her homemade chicken soup, though my appetite was the lowest it would ever be. Lucky for me, she wasn't ready to ask questions. She let me be.

I slept for nearly two days straight until the third day, waking to thoughts of Jim exploding like Pop Rocks in my head. I started to feel panicked, not knowing what was going to become of me. Later in the day, I moseyed out of bed and ventured as far as the porch for a smoke, blankly staring across the yard at the tree line. "Charlene, you best come back inside before you catch cold," Mama called out to me. "I'll make you some hot chocolate."

I followed her to the kitchen, down the front hall past the living room that she kept neatly, dusted and polished, in case we had company. I sat like a lump while she heated milk on the stove. She busied herself, never looking directly at me. But when I unthinkingly swept a finger across my swollen eye, she warned me, "Don't touch it, Charlene. Give it time to heal proper-like." She mixed in the cocoa and a couple of marshmallows and set down the mug on the pinewood table in front of me. "You smell like cigarettes. That's not ladylike." I was going to talk back but didn't have the strength.

Mama went on to her Wednesday night Bible study and left me to fend for myself for food. I made a ham sandwich, scarfed it, then went out to smoke again. I stood stiff but for one leg shaking like a rattle, hoping it wouldn't creep up the rest of my body. My mind was only talking to me about Jim: How was he getting fed? Was he eating that crap food they served at the bar? He didn't go to no store. Not like I fed him all that well myself, but the freezer was full of TV dinners, and he never had to think about it. That's when the phone rang. I ran inside, hitting my knee on the foot rest by the side table where the portable sat, begging in my heart for it to be him. "Hello?" I answered.

"Charlie!" It was my friend, Angela. "Oh my God, girl! I heard you was in the hospital and that it was real bad this time."

"You heard what?" I was half-there listening as the rest of me broke off into shards of disappointment at my feet.

"Oh my gawd. Are you okay? Honey, Jim ain't nothin' but a piece of lousy dog shit. If that was me, my brother would have likely kilt him already...oh...." She fell dead quiet realizing what she'd said, knowing that my brother Danny wasn't anywhere to be found and how close he and I had been. Angela and I had been friends since we could walk, and I knew she was sorry she'd said it.

"I'm okay, Ang. Mama came to get me Sunday night."

"Well, I didn't find out nothin' until yesterday at Maw-Maw's." Maw-Maw's was a country kitchen off Highway 76 up the road from the tire place. "I hadn't been to that place to eat in about three weeks, but I got a hankerin' for her chicken fried steak supper about four in the afternoon, if you can believe it. You wouldn't believe what you crave when you're pregnant." Silence followed. "Shit, Charlie. Shit. I'm sorry."

"You're how far along now?" I managed to get out, both my losses brought up without her saying, the loss of my brother and a baby. The latter was a loss I didn't know about until I had soaked the mattress of the bed I was on in the emergency room after one of Jim's beatings.

"I'm fifteen damn weeks now. Can you fucking believe it? Shit. Well, now Charlie, I wished I had known earlier. I would've come to the hospital. You know I would've."

"I know, Ang. It ain't so bad." I hated the pity I heard in her voice. Made me feel ashamed. She'd found a good man, Lamar Earle Jr. She'd gotten a Junior, too, but he'd come from better stock than my Jimmy. Hers ran the local hardware store and despite being a bit on the religious side, which Angela was not, he loved her so much. He never drank and never hit his wife. And when she met him and started having babies, her pill obsession disappeared like she'd been exorcised.

"It wasn't so bad...been through worse." I tried to sound convincing as I headed out to the porch to where I'd left my cigarettes.

I started feeling weak and nauseous as she went on, "I heard that Jim's daddy's the one who took you to the hospital. Now, I could hardly believe that!"

"Jim's daddy?" I didn't think I'd heard her straight.

"Yeah, they said he stopped by your trailer and found you passed out cold on the kitchen floor. Saw your face all mashed up and took you in. Said you was unconscious."

I couldn't believe that that nasty man would give a minute to help me. I figured it was only because his son was the one responsible and that he was protecting the Wilson name and the reputation of his tire business. Wouldn't look too good having a wife killer for a son. "I'm comin' by tomorrow to see you," Angela went on, "after work. I get off at three. Don't you go back, Charlie."

"I'm not going back," I said in what was more a whisper. I felt so much shame and was confused like the two were playing tag in my head while my stomach was making it hard to hold down the chewed contents of my sandwich.

I put the phone down and took the last hit on my cigarette, which had become nothing but a stumpy thing in my fingers. I started bawling like they do in the movies when they find out somebody's died. I missed Jim so much.

I couldn't stop. I'd see him clean shaven, dark hair gelled back, crystal-blue eyes like aquamarine birthstones. Jealousy brought in Tonya with her long bleach-blond hair, size-two butt, and red fuck-me pumps saddled up beside him in my mind, giving me the "what are you gonna do" look. She was a Tank's deer fly.

My mind went from worrying about what he was eating to who he was fucking, like a hive of wasps moving to the next tree branch. I was close to dry heaving, the thought of him and some woman like Tonya together. Head spinning, I was filling up with a rage like an uncontrolled forest fire. I felt locked in by the darkness and the panic gripped me tight around my neck. There wasn't enough weed to save me from the violent flames fear had set my mind to burn in.

I sobbed for God knows how long after getting off the phone with Angela. I made my way to the bed and threw myself across it. I had thoughts that I would call Jim, but was more afraid to do that than to lay there being seared by thoughts of him being without me.

In a daze, I reached beside the bed for the skirt I had had on from leaving the hospital. I scrambled around the pocket for the piece of paper Nurse Donna had left for me. I dialed the number she'd written not knowing what time it was, nor who the hell I was calling.

A groggy voice on the other end answered, "Yellow!"

I blurted out, "My name's Charlie. Nurse Donna gave me this number. Told me it was all right to call." There was a brief pause and then I heard the man who'd answered hand the phone to someone else.

"This is Shirley," a woman said.

"My name's Charlie. Nurse Donna said it was all right to call..." I repeated myself.

"Well, hi there. Charlie, you said it was?" I could hear this Shirley lady moving around, sheets being ruffled and her breathing telling me she was shifting weight getting out of bed. "So, Charlie. You safe right now?"

"Yes, Ma'am," I replied. "Sorry if it's late." I didn't know what else to say to her—a complete stranger.

"Perfectly all right. So, did Nurse Donna mention the women's group at all?"

"She just...she left me this number...well, the note said that I could...."

"Sure. Sure. Yes, glad you called. So, how about I come pick you up tomorrow around five-thirty and you can come to a meeting with me?"

"Well, uh, I...I'm supposed to meet a friend tomorrow," I stuttered knowing that my plans with Angela never were set in concrete. Never.

"Now, dear, you must be feeling pretty bad to have called me, a woman you don't know. I understand. But I'm sure your friend will understand, too, if you make other arrangements just for tomorrow. I figure you've been going through quite a bit lately." She said all that with a voice that could convince a cat not to lick itself. She was right. I gave her the address to Mama's house wondering what in the world I was going to tell Mama what with some strange lady pulling up in the yard tomorrow.

One thing I clearly remember is that when I got off the phone with Shirley, the jagged, piercing thoughts of Jim without me went soft to nothing. I fell asleep before Mama got home from Bible Study.

6

The next day, Shirley pulled up in a bright red Nissan long-bed at the bottom of our half-a-mile driveway where I stood waiting by the road. I didn't want Mama seeing, because I'd lied about where I was off to. "Where you goin' again?" she'd asked for the tenth time in less than three hours.

"Angela's pickin' me up. God, Mama. You know Angela."

"Charlene Louise. Do you have to take the dear Lord's name in vain? Did I not raise you right for nothin'?" She said all that while barely looking at me. She always seemed focused on something else, either the timer on the oven or the pleat on the skirt she was ironing. But no matter, because I didn't know what the real weight of her worry would be if she ever did look me right in the eye, as banged up as mine was. "She best not be taking you to see Jim is all."

"Mama. I'd done told you. She hates him worse than you." She looked just passed me, steady, then to the ceiling.

"Jesus forgive her. Hate is a cruel word. Never as long as I lived have I had hate in my heart. We are all God's children." I'd made her mad, obviously, but it worked as far as getting her to stop being so concerned over where I was going so I could make my way to the end of our drive.

I'd only made it halfway through a cigarette when Shirley, a woman I didn't know who'd convinced me with few words to let her pick me up and take me to an unknown location, was stopped in front of me. I stomped it out in the dirt by my feet, took a deep breath, and hopped in. She had what sounded like Indian flute music playing from the truck stereo, and

I seriously considered telling her I wasn't feeling so good. By the looks of her, though, I could tell she wouldn't have bought it. "Nice to meet you in person, Charlie," she said as she shifted to second.

"Same to you," I replied, nervous as I'd ever been in light of something I cared about. Of course, I didn't know that at the time. It had been so long that the only thing I cared about was Jim. I couldn't remember the last time I had done something for myself. All I knew then was that I wasn't jumping out of a moving truck. I wasn't running, scared or not.

"Do you have any younguns?" she asked. A laugh slipped out from my mouth before I could stop it, and I felt red with shame from being so rude. She must have been able to tell, because she didn't press. "Well, Charlie, you must be curious as to where I'm taking you!"

"A little," I admitted.

"Well, I thought as much," she answered plainly. She reached over to turn down the music, and I stole a peek at her. She looked to be in her mid-fifties with shoulder-length gray hair, and a deep red shawl around her shoulders. She wore large, brown glasses like everybody wore in the Eighties. "I thought you might wanna know where you're going," she said again, giggling a little as if she was excited to be sharing a special secret with me. "You know Bethel Lutheran? The little church on Main?"

"That the one with the red doors?"

"Sure is. That's it."

"I know of it," I replied and then she got serious while telling me how a group of "us" get together once a week and meet in the basement of "that" church. A tightness filled my chest while finding it a struggle to swallow after the mention of word "group". She had mentioned a "meeting" last night, but I was so tired and relieved to have gotten ahold of someone that I had paid it little mind. "I'm not really into talking to a whole bunch of people," I managed to mumble.

"Well, you most certainly don't have to say a thing. You can just listen. They're good women."

"Are you going to stay?" I asked her, sounding like the little girl who'd asked Danny to stay with her in the dark.

"Of course. I started that meeting fifteen years ago. Have barely missed a week since, myself," she replied, steering us down the highway nearing the edge of town.

"Is it a prayer meeting?" I asked, now more curious to what I was in for, even though it seemed like there was no turning back.

"Shucks no. Well, not really. No. We do pray, sort of. God is a part of it. But this ain't about Jesus nor religion."

Hearing this woman, Shirley, use the word "ain't" was like hearing a teacher use it, and I took it to mean that she wasn't fooling me. But I found it mighty hard to believe that a group of women meeting in a church and praying to not have anything to do with Christ himself. I didn't see how that was possible at all. And I knew that my mama's poor heart would stutter-beat hearing of such talk.

We pulled behind the church to the back parking lot. The lights were on in one of the basement windows. A couple of other cars pulled up then, too.

One woman, who I quickly learned was named Willow, was an overly excited regular whose job in life it seemed to be was to welcome everybody. She pulled up waving feverishly with one hand, all the while talking to somebody in the seat next to her. Before she even got the car door closed, she began shouting at Shirley. "Hi, Shirley! Honey! So glad to see you. Got somebody I want you to meet."

The stumpy, plain woman who was riding shotgun like me moseyed alongside her, eyes just looking down at her feet. So I'm the not the only one doesn't got a clue about being here, I thought. Before I could ask, Shirley was walking towards Willow and the other newbie. I took out a cigarette and hung back by the truck. Shirley looked back at me and gave me a nod meaning it was all right and she wouldn't go in without me.

Willow seemed more curious about me and stared in my direction all the while patting the scared woman beside her. I wondered if she could see my bruised eye from there. I was glad Shirley hadn't said anything about it, because I was nervous enough without having to explain my condition. I only got a few drags in before I got the signal it was time to head inside.

I want to say I remember something somebody said that day, but it's not clear; my mind was such a wreck. I may have remembered Willow welcoming me, but then I think that came to light only later. When you're numb your whole life, you don't come to all at once. At least I didn't.

§

"If you're gonna stay under my roof, Charlene Louise, you best be straight with me. The Lord does not take kindly to a lying tongue and neither do I," Mama said, scolding me as soon as I was less than both feet in the front door. Shit. Angela had called asking for me. I'd forgotten to give her a heads up.

"Why must you make a spectacle of me like that? Tellin' me you was goin' to be with Angela." She was hopping mad but spoke all that as calmly as if she was asking if she could get me a glass of milk. "Oh, you can make a fool of me, but you can't make a fool of the Lord. No, ma'am." Her drawn-on eyebrows were furrowed and her lips pursed so tight the words, though even, squeezed their escape out of her mouth.

She had a plate of chicken and green beans and dinner rolls on the table. She'd let them get cold. "I didn't tell you where I was going, Mama, because I didn't want you to worry," I replied, knowing it was useless.

"Oh, so telling me you were somewhere you wasn't was to help me not worry 'bout you? When did lyin' become the carin' thing to do? Jesus didn't lie to his people, and they had lots more to worry about."

"Mama, please," I mumbled. I was spent, and I couldn't take her arguing about how Jesus and his people suffered more than anyone else ever had. To her it was simple. If Jesus did it the way he did with all he went through, then surely the rest of us could buck it up.

To me, it was a little different, because I don't know how many times Jesus got himself put in the hospital by the love of his life. And I don't know what Jesus knew about desire and desperation. What did he know about the need that claws at your insides and scratches your nerves to the core until the only thing left to do is to go back to the man that hates more days than he loves, you included?

So, before I knew it, before I could help myself, I said to her, "You didn't have to leave, Mama. Daddy left. He left you and me and Danny, so you didn't have to!" I shouted mean truths at her until I saw water droplets form in the corners of her eyes and her lips break, quivering. Her shoulders began shaking like I'd never seen before, and she walked straight to the kitchen table, picked up my plate of cold food and dumped every last bit on the floor right at my feet. I crumpled down in a pile like I had in my own kitchen less than a week before as she turned around and walked out.

I cried and cried until I was hyperventilating. I wanted to see, not Jim then, but my brother. I wished he would walk in and put his arms around me and shush me and tell me it'd be all right. I wished he would come make it better for me and Mama. And through my pity and sorrow, with no Daddy, no Danny, and no Jim, I called out— weak, but utterly surrendered, "God. Oh God. Please, help me."

I remember one time when I went to church with Mama, back when I was eight or sometime before my Daddy died, sitting through the longest sermon on record. It wasn't that long sermons were unusual, but this one stood out because Mama had made me wear a pair of green tights that matched my green corduroy dress, the neck lined with tiny red flowers. I've never been a dress girl. It was for Mama. And I hated wearing tights more than I would hate sleeping in a sandbox. That green pair weren't long enough, so there was a huge gap between the crotch of the tights and my own.

We sat there for what seemed like more time than it took for God to make the Earth and all the creatures in it as Pastor Eppleby rambled on and on about nothing I gave two worn-out pennies about. All I ever cared about in church was singing the hymns, which I kept to myself ever since Danny shamed me for singing my first "Hallelujah."

Mama wouldn't stand for wiggling, and my butt got to itching from sitting on the hardest slab of wood to ever make a pew for what felt like an eternity. I got to where I couldn't take it any longer. Pastor Eppleby paused, and I thought he was going to finally stop talking so we could all go home and I could get those damn skin-itchers off. Turns out, he wasn't near finished and that may be when it first occurred to me that there was no way Jesus suffered worse than we did. I knew in my heart Jesus was never made to wear tights that didn't fit and sit his bony butt down in a hard wooden pew from hours on end being bored to tears.

As Pastor Eppleby's sermon rolled on, I got to feeling hotter and hotter, which made me start to cry. My guess now was I was having a panic attack, but I didn't know that back then. I started sobbing and couldn't stop for nothing. People started to turn around and look at Mama who was fumbling for a tissue in her purse. Tall, older Mr. Henckle, who looked like a living skeleton, turned around and offered me his hanky. My mama, much obliged, took the hanky and handed it to me. I was so embarrassed and knowing what I was doing to her only made it worse. So I cried more.

My brother, turns out, thought my coming apart was right funny and started to snicker. Before I knew it, my crying turned into hysteria. I glanced at him for a mere second, caught the joke in his eyes and burst out laughing louder than a singing choir of angels. The congregation started paying more attention to the Montgomery family than poor Pastor Eppleby and his Jesus talk, so he decided it was a good time to wrap it up before losing us all.

It was too late for Danny and me, and Mama knew it. She jerked me up by my elbow, while hissing at my brother, "Come. Now." She yanked me down the side aisle toward the door that led to the church basement stairwell and out to the back parking lot with my brother not but a half-step behind.

"Get in the car," she snapped, not looking either one of us in the eye. For some reason, whatever had possessed me and my brother in the sanctuary left as soon as we were alone with her. "Wait 'til your Daddy hears about this," was all she said. I didn't believe she would tell him, though, because she didn't like to make him mad when he wasn't. No matter. The ride back to our house was awful quiet, but I didn't care so much. I knew those horrible green tights would soon be coming off.

§

The next week, Shirley picked me up again. This time she came up the drive. I got into the cab next to her. I could see Mama peeking out of the sitting room window. I knew she was curious as to who Shirley was and what sort of thing I was going to be saying to her about Mama and our family.

Honest to God, later, when I finally confessed as to where I'd been and what went on in that church basement, she said, "You know, Charlene, it's prideful to talk about yourself. Just prideful." It was impossible to convince her that I hadn't jumped right in to talking about her messed-up relationship with my daddy, telling her secrets.

"I didn't say nothin'."

"So, nobody didn't ask you questions?"

"Mama," I replied, dulled by her talking around what she was getting at. And I knew she wanted to know the names of those women who had the indecency to talk about their problems with other women.

How could I tell her how comforting it was to be with them, even though most of me was barely there? My head was full of thoughts of Jim and my heart leaked for missing him so, but I was more afraid that they would want me to talk about my life and worst of all, him. I knew, however, that I would continue to go to the meeting, as long as Shirley came to get me. I'd be going and Mama would have to accept it.

Shirley talked most of the way to town over the same Indian flute music as the week before. Of course it could have been completely different with all I knew about Indian music—being nothing. She told me that George was nothing like her first husband, trying to relay some hope. She said her first husband had been a pots and pans salesman, traveling all over the United States. She said, too, he was the son of a friend of her father's and said it was obsession at first sight. She told me his name was Ronald but she called him Ronnie. And even though he was on the road almost thirty-two weeks out of the year, his being home was some of the most brutal moments of her life. She said if he'd been gone only thirty-one weeks, he'd have killed her.

There was a darkness that seemed to cross over her face as she talked of this Ronnie fellow. It was as if the Indian flute playing, gray-haired, smock-wearing mountain woman had the history of being a street junkie.

I never saw it like that for me with Jim until I saw it hang on Shirley's face in her truck on our way to that meeting. The awareness of the insanity of what my desperation was like sent chills up my arms. I sat there in shock. In less than ten minutes, I was relating to this woman who I hardly knew better than I'd ever related to my own kin.

A whole bucketful of questions rushed through my head. Would I look like I was on drugs if I were to talk about Jim? Hell. Did I look like that when I was just thinking about him? It was as if somebody had put a loudspeaker up to my ear and started playing the Talk About Jim Radio Show - Tell Us How You Really Feel, Charlie. The worst part was I couldn't seem to switch the channel or even turn down the volume.

The only break I got was when I was at the meeting the week before, when it seemed to give me something I'd not had, ever. I didn't know what to call it. Aside from the brief moment when Shirley was talking about her ex-old man, she and those women looked to have relief from the demon. Relief. That's what I wanted.

It was the second week's meeting that I remembered more than the first. Willow, the really happy one, not to my surprise remembered me just fine. She greeted me as though I was someone told they would never walk again only to be walking without a hitch the very next day. There was another newbie with her, not the same as before. I overheard Willow mention that she had missed a phone call from the previous newbie and then I saw she didn't look as cheery as she was explaining how she hadn't heard from that girl since.

She introduced her "Newbie of the Week," as I began calling Willow's people she brought once I became a regular. The woman's name was Elizabeth Ann, and she wasn't originally from Eden's Gap. She had gray-speckled, short brown hair and small wire-framed glasses perched on her sharply angled nose. If she hadn't come with Willow, I would've sworn someone from the church had sent her in to counsel us crazy mountain folk. She dressed so conservative and neat in a shirt so starched, I stared at her wondering how she managed to bend her arms to ever scratch her nose or wipe her butt.

The first part of the meeting was set aside for those of us who were new to say something. I could barely say my name. But Elizabeth Ann, who sounded weak and timid like a broken-winged bird downed right outside a yard full of barn cats, well, she went right on introducing herself and telling part of her story. Turns out she met her husband at a university they worked at together. His mama had gotten sick and they'd moved here to be closer to her until she died from colon cancer.

When Elizabeth Ann paused less than a second, Willow practically shouted, "Welcome, Elizabeth Ann! You are never alone again!" I thought it was funny since they'd ridden together. She handed Elizabeth Ann a tissue, because by that point she had tears streaming down her cheeks, fogging up her glasses.

Through sniffles, she went on to tell us how she had ended up taking care of both her husband and his mama. I'd never heard of them, last name Peterson, probably because they lived in town in a giant house where people with money lived.

She said he couldn't handle the fact that his mama was dying and fell into a depression marked with heavy drinking and blasts of rage. She said, too, that his violence spanned about twenty-five years of their marriage, with it getting worse when his mama fell ill.

I couldn't believe that someone could live like that for that long. Plus, she must have been smart since she was a professor and she had still picked a mean husband. That shocked me the most. Even though me and this librarian-looking woman had lots of differences in our stories, we had some things in common, too, just like I had realized in the car with Shirley. What

I would learn in time was that I was starting to identify.

After Elizabeth Ann finished sharing and everyone thanked her, Shirley led us into the main part of the meeting, saying we would focus on gratitude. I thought the group had some loose marbles, wanting to talk about being grateful after what Elizabeth Ann had just cried about to everybody. I was finding it hard to think of a thing to be grateful about.

I did have one thought that seemed kind of like gratitude and that was that I wasn't one of those starving African kids on TV with the flies buzzing 'round them like trash left to rot. I had never not eaten in my life. Aside from that, the only gratitude I knew of was when Jim would make it home, and I could breathe again.

What threw me about the way the women talked about gratitude that night was how not one of them talked about it like I had ever thought about it, the ways I was thinking about it. Nobody said, "He hit me like this," or "I went to the hospital five times," or "Had to have full dental work by the age of forty, but at least I'm still alive." They talked about gratitude like waking up in the morning and being able to make the bed, or enjoying a cup of coffee by a warm fire, or being able to call another woman from the group and say "Hello" and "How are you?" They talked about how it was to wake up and not miss or hate the man that tortured not only their bodies but their hearts as well.

§

While I was deep in thought about what I'd just witnessed, this new way of looking at my life, Shirley was at the wheel humming. She interrupted herself. "You know, Charlie, it's important to have a topic for discussion." She went on to say how it was a way of providing structure, a guidepost, even if people didn't strictly adhere to it. She adjusted her glasses as she looked across the dash, eyes on the road. Then she added, "There are no defined rules. Only suggestions. We've been told what and how enough."

I can't say I remember Jim telling me too much what and how, because he was hardly around to boss me. What I mostly got, when he was there, was him putting me down or making fun of me. He talked to me like I didn't count, like I wasn't a person. I suppose that could be considered the same.

"What do I gotta do?" I asked her.

"You got to believe in miracles," she replied, "Even for you." She winked at me.

Oh my Lord, I thought. What kind of answer is that? Believe in miracles. At least I had somebody to ask questions to, I reminded myself—that was something. That was enough then. That was until I was back at Mama's, alone in my room, and the small break I had gotten from being at the meeting and in the truck with Shirley seemed to ease away from me like the going out of the ocean tide.

8

The next day, I woke up feeling like somebody had ripped my guts out. It'd been a measly two weeks since I got out of the hospital, and I was missing Jim bad. Attending the meeting with Shirley each week helped squelch the craving a bit, a tiny bit. But the gnawing came back strong—fierce in me as soon as I'd opened my eyes.

Luckily, I'd agreed to help Mama prepare for one of her prayer circles that day, so I had to pull it together enough to get myself out of bed. One of the local couples had lost their youngest and the church ladies got together to plan meals and to pray. I couldn't imagine going through the grief of losing a child. I'd only been a few months in, the doctor said four, that time. It wasn't like I'd given birth and held her, night after night. I felt sad for these people I didn't know.

I was curious how prayer worked in a situation like that, too. I'd only known of the one case when it did something useful. I was fifteen at the time, and one of Danny's friends, Tad, had been in a bad car accident. He'd been driving home through the mountains when a flash flood surrounded him. Downpours and water ran over the road in huge sheets. Lightning crackled through the sky and thunder rattled his bones. I think Tad was one of the good kids, too. Decent. Not a druggie like Danny would later be. In fact, the story is that he'd gone to pick up milk and bread for his mama and on his way back the sky broke, so he was blind behind the wheel.

He slid off the road and hit a tree. He was laid up unconscious in the hospital for almost two months. Mama's church, where he and his family went regular, they got together around his bed and prayed a million "Our Fathers" and whatever healing-to-Jesus prayers there are. They prayed and prayed. The doctor said they didn't know if Tad would be okay, even if he did come to from the coma, because of the trauma to his brain.

Mama's church prayed anyway. Now, according to her, you're not really supposed to pray for anything but for the good Lord to do his will in all matters. If what God wants is what is going to happen, then I thought why bother praying at all? But she said if people come together in Jesus's holy name and praise God's goodness, then you've got more of a chance for God to grant one of his miracles.

Now, I know that Tad's mama prayed that God would bring a miracle to her son, and I knew it was more about what she wanted than praising the goodness of God who put her son in the coma in the first place. So, it was all hard for me to wrap my mind around. I mean, if heaven was so great and Jesus so special, then wouldn't she be beside herself that God was close to removing her loved one from this hellhole and returning him to His heavenly side?

I wasn't sure all the church-going folk, including my mama, were so convinced heaven is as wonderful as is written and glorified. To my way of figuring, if it was so, wouldn't their prayers be more for Him granting the true miracle, removal from this not-so-great life and deliverance to the far-better afterlife, side by side with Jesus?

At the end of months of praying for Tad, Mama and her do-gooders were getting weary because the number of people showing up to the hospital was getting thin. But out of nowhere, one Tuesday afternoon, "God's wondrous ways did He perform." Tad's eyes popped open and he cried out, "Mama! Mama! I forgot something at the store. I have to go back."

According to my own mama, who had relentlessly stayed by her church sister's side, Tad's mama passed out cold when he came to. While the nurses and doctors filed in, pushing Mama and Tad's mama into the hall so they could run checks on the boy, Mama said they both felt the presence of the Lord. Right outside of his room, they praised Jesus for his merciful love. Maybe Jesus is merciful in that he knows what people don't—maybe heaven's not all that great, either.

§

Mama and me went to her church, the Mount Tabor, after having stopped by the Ingles for extra items, "Just in case Lou Anne or Coralee forgot something." Standing at the back of the Sable in the church parking lot, I let her pile two full bags of groceries on me to carry inside.

I followed Mama through the sanctuary to the basement to where five other church ladies would be making cheese biscuits, tuna casserole, and macaroni and cheese for the grieving young couple. I didn't know how they coordinated that sort of thing, but I thought we might have brought too much. I'd wanted to argue with Mama but was finding it too tiring. I'd kept my mouth shut.

My nerves were frayed from thinking about Jim. My obsession was growing bigger, not smaller, even though I had been taking the directions Shirley gave me: journaling, saying the Serenity Prayer. I hadn't called any of the other women, but I had scribbled my darkest thoughts and feelings and mumbled the stupid prayer, though I believed in prayer as much as I believed in the sanctity of heaven. It didn't seem to be working. The wall I'd had, the one keeping me from losing my mind, shabby as it was to begin with, was getting to be completely useless. I was jonesing for my husband, and I was jonesing bad.

As soon as Mama and I entered the sanctuary (I think she took me that way on purpose), it dawned on me that my mind had turned to sex. The red carpet on the floor and lining of the cushions of the pews reminded me of how I didn't belong in a holy place and how guilty of sinning I was. The last time I had been in church was Easter before I'd dropped out of high school. That was when Mama got Danny and me to go out of guilt.

She had bought me a special white dress, with more flowers and lace and puffy sleeves. Mama'd bought Danny a new tie. I never wore dresses, and he never wore ties. I felt awkward and silly but kept the dress on because she'd spent money on us, and my brother told me I looked pretty. He said it was nice that I would try and look like a girl rather than my usual jeans, t-shirt, and man's oversized flannel button-down. I told him he looked handsome, rather than his usual t-shirt, jeans and men's oversized flannel button-down. I meant it. He told me to fuck off, then punched me lightly on my puff-covered shoulder.

Later that day, when I was with Jim, he laughed in my face saying I looked like a "goddamn child" in that "stupid thing." "Look at you, Miss Pure and Holy. Praise Jesus," he snorted at me. I was foolish to think Jim would ever say anything sweet. Didn't matter that he shamed me, because he still enjoyed pulling that same dress up, my panties down and fucking me.

Deep down, I must've started to put the two together, him shaming me and then wanting me. I wasn't aware of it, of course. There must have been a switch in my mind that got flipped, because I took his way of teasing as if it wasn't mean. It's when I got his attention, which I craved. My mind turned it inside out, like making something bad be good.

As we made our way toward the back of the church, Mama said, louder than usual, "I remember the day you were baptized." It was as if she was letting Jesus know that she'd tried to do her part.

"Yeah, felt like I was being drowned in front of everybody," I said, it slipping from my mouth, knowing I'd probably made God upset as soon as I'd set foot in the door, just adding to my list. At that, Mama spun around, looked at me, the glare casting a dark shadow across her powdered pale face.

"Do not start, Charlene Louise Montgomery. Not in His house." When she used my whole name, I knew I'd better act straight. We walked to the front through the side door to the left of the pulpit, down the stairs to the basement, the same route she took escorting Danny and me out that Sunday I lost my sense wearing those green itchy tights.

"Sorry," I managed. For the first time in a long time, I had the feeling of not wanting to be difficult. It was then that I knew I needed to be doing something besides sitting home wondering, and I couldn't think of a better distraction, other than getting loaded, than to be with my mama and her church friends. I hadn't smoked anything since I'd been back at her house. I was too afraid it'd remind me of being in the trailer. That was a miracle in itself, but I knew I wasn't going to be able to hold on for too much longer.

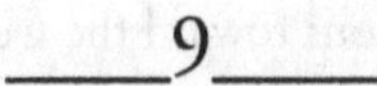

9

The morning after helping Mama at church, I woke up from a sleep filled with raggedy dreams that didn't make any sense, except for leaving an achy residue in every crevice of my body. One minute, they had me in Mama's living room and the next I'd be in our trailer by Jimmy's folks. I couldn't make heads or tails of them, but I was remembering them clearer than some of my waking life memories.

In one from that night, I was standing in front of a mirror, my face black and blue as if I'd gone through another round of beatings from Jim. I'd try to speak, and right as I'd start to say something, nothing but smoke would come out of my mouth. Smoke was pouring out and the next thing, it was as if that mirror wasn't a mirror anymore but had become a window. I could see back into the woods where I had been running that night in the hospital.

I hadn't remembered much from my dream in the hospital until that one. When I woke up I remembered that I had been running, about naked, tripping, the cave, wolf-like woman, the fire and all. I thought I'd better talk to Shirley. She listened to all that flute music. Maybe she had weird dreams, too, and would know what they meant or what to do. I hadn't told anybody about what I'd seen in the hospital, but maybe she would understand that or else I'd have to admit I was losing my mind after all.

I sat up, feeling over the edge of the bed for my socks on the floor. I slipped them on and got up. I went over to my dresser, felt for my pack of smokes and lighter tucked underneath my one sweatshirt and extra panties in the top drawer. It wasn't but 5:30 in the morning, and I was wide awake and already thinking too much. It was too early to call Shirley. I didn't feel like journaling or praying, neither.

I took my favorite flannel shirt, hanging over the door, put it on and headed outside. It was cold and dark. I could see the moon behind a blanket of clouds. I wished I had a cup of coffee but didn't want to wake Mama. I stood there staring out toward the woods, much the same way I'd stared into the mirror-turned-window in my dream, when I remembered something else from it.

It was Jim. In the dream, I'd walked through the mirror and into the woods, because I was looking for something. I'd made it not more than twenty feet when I walked into a thick pile of God knows what, until I saw that it was him. He was curled up in a ball on the ground, in leaves and decomposing wood chips. I bent down to look closer at him, thrilled that I'd found him. But then I didn't know what to do. He was sleeping, and though I wanted more than anything to talk to him, I was afraid that if I woke him, he'd get mad and leave.

I couldn't help but reach out to touch his shoulder as gently as I could. Then I touched his hair and started to reach for his face. The rest was blurry. I was annoyed. I wanted, I needed, to remember more of him.

My fingers and toes had started going numb from being outside in the cold. I put out my cigarette and turned to go back inside, even more unsure what to do with myself in that moment—feeling endless and unstoppable.

It suddenly dawned on me: What kind of wife doesn't try to make things right with her husband? Sure, he hadn't called me, either. What kind of a husband doesn't try and call his wife? Didn't he care? Oh my God. What if Jim didn't even care?

My stomach lurched inside toward my chest. I headed to the bathroom. I needed to hurry. Mama would be up soon.

I washed my face quickly, put on some makeup, pulled my hair back in a scrunchie and sprayed my bangs. Luckily, Mama still kept her keys on the same little hook next to the kitchen door my brother had hung for her.

With keys in hand, thankful to not have heard a peep from her room, I was on my way back to my husband. In the car, I began to picture what I might find. Maybe my gurgling stomach was trying to tell me something. I swallowed and breathed deeply. As I turned out of the drive, I had a feeling of being on a boat going down a swell. And then the boat smacked head on into a wave as soon as I had the thought, he could be home and not alone.

The sun was coming up and beams of dull winter sun hit Mama's dirty windshield making it hard to see. I knew that road as good as I knew how loneliness felt, so it didn't slow me down any. When I got to the tire place, I pulled around back, hopeful, ready to start over with Jim. I was ready to get my husband back.

The crash of another wave smacked me in the face as his truck wasn't out front of the trailer, and though his folks lived a ways back, I could see his truck wasn't parked up there, neither. I should've known better. I should've known that he couldn't be alone, and he sure as all hell wasn't going to be going to his mama for comforting because his wife was gone.

I felt like somebody had told me Jim was dead. It was as if I had been knocked clean out of my boat, left to fight for breath as if I was being pushed under water sinking deeper and deeper, my lungs filling up fast.

I opened the car door just in time to not throw up all over the inside of Mama's car. I heaved as if I was coughing up shards of what had been hope, retching its way out.

I got out of the car, stepping over my own vomit, and ran up to the front door of our trailer. It was locked. I tried to force it open, banging it with my fists.

As I was beating on the door, I was hollering Jim's name at the top of my lungs. I could hear Rosco, his parents' Blue Tick, up the way barking like mad at all the racket I was making. Blind fury had taken over me. I hit the glass on the door so hard I broke it without noticing a gaping cut on my hand.

Seems like the Devil's mistress had taken over my body and he himself was directing my mind because I broke into my own trailer, headed to the bedroom, tore through some of Jim's clothes in the side drawer and retrieved his pistol. I found myself back in Mama's car tearing off down the road toward the house of the only person I hated worse than the evils of meth that had taken my brother. Of all the women that hung around Tank's, most of them missing more than a tooth, there was one who came from decent folks from a decent side of town. Meredith Hussey, supposedly pronounced "Hoo-say" like it was French. To me, she was a hussey, pure and simple and her name fit her more than her upbringing. She had perfect teeth and had bleached her hair blond since the days of the bonfire up on Mill Mountain Road. She'd always been and would always be a whore for my husband, and it was her house I was headed for.

There's something I'd learn about later, and that is a thing Shirley would talk to me about quite a bit, as well as some of the other ladies from my meetings—divine intervention. It's when a person starts unraveling and is about to really mess things up for themselves, but in special cases God steps in on that person's behalf and saves them from killing themselves or somebody else.

You see, as I was about to turn down Maple Street toward the slut's quaint yellow house with its white picket fence, blue lights flashed behind me. The siren broke the sound barrier of the hollowed out spell that had me behind the wheel of Mama's Mercury Sable.

I stopped the car at the edge of the 100-year-old red oaks that lined the street. A single thought crossed my mind as my eyes gazed over to the passenger seat where the pistol was sitting: One quick shot to the temple like in the movies. Darkness was interrupted by a sharp tapping on my window where an old schoolmate of mine stood in his clean deputy uniform. Deputy Shane Perkins leaned his head forward to make eye contact with me, Shirley standing behind him in her red shawl. Behind both of them, stood my mama. He slowly opened my door, like pulling the lid off a boiling pot, careful of the steam, his hand on his pistol at his side. I looked at them through wads of tears.

Deputy Perkins took his hand from his holster to help escort me to Shirley's truck as Mama repossessed her own car without saying a word. Shirley nodded at her, as if they'd worked out a plan ahead of time and were right on schedule. It was like they were rescuing me from a natural disaster, rather than the disaster I had been about to create.

There wasn't but a couple of folks to come out of their houses, gawking at us, like a freak show festival. That's how Southern people do, anyway. Deputy Perkins waved them back inside. "Nothing to worry about. It's alright."

Nobody mentioned the pistol as I got out of the car. Maybe nobody saw it; maybe I was catching the break of a lifetime.

Shirley assured Deputy Wilson that I would be watched closely back at Mama's. That's when they saw the dried blood on my hand. She reached over quick, grabbing my wrist. "What'd you do, Charlie?" Nobody waited for me to explain. "We'll take care of that at home," she said as she padded around the cut with her thumb. "I'm sure your Mama's got some supplies we can use to fix this right up," she said softly to me, looking me straight in the eyes as if to see I was still there.

"I'll be checkin' in on you, now. Alright?" Deputy Perkins said, helping me in the passenger side of Shirley's truck. He closed the door and continued a conversation without me before Shirley hopped in the other side.

"Girl. God is doing for you what you could not do for yourself," she repeated as we headed up the windy highway. It seemed so quiet without her flute music playing, and as I sat there, I imagined three tiny canoes banked on the shore of some impassible river. I couldn't believe I wasn't in the back of a police car being taken to jail.

I wasn't scared of Jim any more. Not then. I was scared of myself. I was more scared of what I'd been driven to by my own mind than anything Jim had ever done. I had lost all control of me, all control.

§

The rest of that day was a blur. I had been lucky to stumble up the steps into the house, hearing Mama and Shirley talking. Making out bits of what they were saying, as it sounded like they were standing under a blanket, Shirley was telling Mama it was lucky she'd noticed her keys missing when she did. And then Mama thanked Shirley for calling George's nephew, for his help in this "family matter."

They stopped talking when I sat down in the kitchen and together they tended to the cut on my hand. It stung a bit when they poured iodine over it, but lucky for me, or not, I had had worse wounds. They wrapped it like a mummy in a white bandage. When they were done, I went straight to my bedroom to lie down. Mama hadn't been mad at me when we got to the house, which seemed itself like a miracle. I guessed that when He got to performing miracles in one's life, He did them as a set.

10

The next day, my head was killing me. It was as if I'd drank two liters of tequila, forgetting to choke down the worm. The cut on my hand hurt like a son of a bitch. Mama was up by the time I got up, and when I made it to the kitchen, she'd made homemade biscuits with thick pieces of bacon. She handed me a plate, looking at the dark blood that had leaked through.

"We should clean that again."

I nodded and felt sick to my stomach, knowing she wanted me to eat something. I managed to get down a few bites. I wanted to thank her for the previous day, for the breakfast, for everything, without knowing the words to say. She spoke first, "Danny called yesterday afternoon."

"What?" I replied, shocked, my head still throbbing. She was almost going to leave it there, like that, with nothing on what he called about. "Mama," I said firmly.

"Said he's in big trouble, Charlie. Wants me to send him some money. I didn't want to add to your troubles but thought you'd want to know." She spoke so softly I had to stop chewing to hear her.

I hadn't talked to my brother in years but knew what him needing money was all about. And the fact that he'd called her for it, no matter how bad off he was, didn't sound like Danny at all. It sounded wrong, terribly wrong.

I looked at my mama's tiny figure, hands wrapped in her apron matching the scrunched look on her face. "Did he say where he was, Mama?" She didn't answer. She turned to the sink, her hands bracing the edge of the bowl. "You're not gonna send him money, are you?"

I went over to her, wrapped my arms around her. "It's gonna be all right," I told her. "You hear me? We are gonna be all right." I didn't know where that strength and understanding was coming from, but I knew that it was more than plain old me.

"Anyone home?" a voice called from the front porch, faint but becoming more obvious as I unwrapped my arms from Mama. We heard a knock on the front door and a man's voice called out again. Mama stepped away from me, blotted her eyes, took a deep breath in, let it out, then headed toward the front room.

I could hear her let the man in and heard footsteps in the front hall. "Charlene," she called to me. "Would you put the pot on for some coffee? We got us some company."

"Oh Lord," I thought, wondering if it was someone she knew from church. I peeked a look at my reflection in a metal mixing bowl on the counter. Not good. The emotional toil from the day before had me weathered like flood-washed dirt.

I got out the can of Folgers and a filter from the cupboard and filled the CoffeeMate full. "Charlene," she called to me again, quieter than a shout though her voice was raised to get my attention. "Comin'," I called back, making sure not to shout, neither.

§

Most Southerners know that it's disrespectful to yell at your folks, and never, ever in front of company. And most of us don't need to learn what respecting your elders entails, gentle in nature or not. We just know. But if I ever did forget, my brother Danny was sure to make sure to set me straight.

Once, Mama had asked me to hand her her gloves from the side table nearest to me. I tossed them over to her. Danny caught them midair and looked at me stern-like. "Don't throw nothin' at Mama. Ever," he said, his face set tight enough to snap his jaw off. He put the gloves back in my lap, staring at me until I met Mama at the door and handed them to her like he thought was proper.

Danny's seriousness got more so the older we got, usually related to how we were treating Mama. It was like an old man had stolen his shoes. It drove me nutballs, him telling me what to do, but I didn't mess with him. I knew he was trying to make up for Daddy's sorriness and then Daddy being gone. But he couldn't do it for long, as he had to escape, too, in his own way.

When we were young, my brother and I could be silly together. I could be minding my own business when he'd tackle me to the ground and tickle me like he'd been paid $100 to do it. He was relentless until I made so much noise, Mama'd come around scolding us out of panic we'd wake Daddy.

He'd make faces at me every chance he got. Church was his favorite place, like the Sunday of the green tights, trying to get me to the point of no return. I never knew anybody but Danny who could scrunch their eyebrows and lips to their nose like those wrinkle dogs. "Your face is gonna get stuck like that and you'll never get married," I'd holler.

"Good! Marriage is gross!" he'd reply.

§

I walked heavy-footed to the front room to meet our guest. As I got nearer and could see into the room, I saw Mama sitting as still as a wide-opened clam, resting at the bottom of the ocean, listening to Deputy Shane Perkins ramble on about something or another. What is it about men? How did they have such power to pull us in, even if we could care less what they're actually saying? He finished his sentence and stood as I stepped out of the hallway. "Hi, Charlie."

"Shane," I replied, half embarrassed and half not caring, for what he'd seen of me the day before. "Coffee's almost ready."

"Oh. I won't be here that long." With that, I could see disappointment move like the shadow of a plane across Mama's face.

"Now, Deputy Perkins. Don't be in such a hurry. Please, set a while," she politely urged, the happy clam closing.

The presence of a gentle man in her house was like fresh rain after a muggy day. The air was easier to breathe in. Just then a beep went off in the kitchen. She sprung up, looking relieved. "How do you like your coffee, son?" she asked him.

"Just black is fine, ma'am," he said. She left me alone with him, standing there awkwardly, like a bird with one leg. I was still in a bit of a fog, so I was finding conversation hard to make.

Shane seemed relaxed just fine. He wasn't in his uniform as he was the day before but was wearing a loose, brown t-shirt and jeans. His hair was a thick one-color, also brown like a shoe. He parted it in the middle, brushing short bangs straight in the front.

"I just wanted to see how you're doing today," he said, looking at the wrapping on my hand. I could feel the blood rise up my neck and the moistening of my palms. I wasn't able to remember when's the last time a man considered me at all.

"Fine. Thanks," I managed, waving the bandage lightly as evidence.

"Your mama was worried about you yesterday," he said, his even tone saying more like, "I knew you were heading toward real trouble if we hadn't come along." I was relieved when Mama walked in with our coffees. She had his in a mug I'd never seen before. It had a buck's head on the side of it, as if the deer was hanging from a wall like a trophy. It seemed to fit Deputy Shane's large, rough hands, but I couldn't remember it being around when Daddy was alive.

Mama handed me a cup in her pink roses china. Delicate was never a description applied to me, but I loved her china. She'd gotten mixed floral pieces from the local thrift store, some more purple, some more peach colored. The one she handed me was mauve, and secretly my favorite. "Thank you, Mama," I said, then took a sip. The coffee was perfect, and I needed a smoke.

"Wanna step outside?" I asked him, knowing Mama was going to head quickly back to the kitchen. I knew, too, that she was thinking how unladylike it was for me to smoke front of a "suitor." After what he'd witnessed from me the day before, I didn't think him seeing me smoke was going to be the turnoff.

Mama wrung her hands by her side but smiled at the both of us before leaving us standing there by ourselves.

"A smoke?" I asked him. Deputy Shane grabbed his jacket and followed me out to the porch. "So, how long have you been a deputy?" I asked, putting a fresh white Marlboro to my lips, the clean tobacco smell running up my nose. Before I could reach my lighter, he pulled a black Bic from his jacket and extended me a light.

I leaned back against the railing, him less than arm's length away, as he lit himself a cigarette, too. Then he launched into telling me the story of his life after high school. He'd always wanted to be a police officer, he told me. And like most of us, couldn't wait to finish high school so he could do what he really wanted to do. I exhaled off to the side. It was nice to hear someone talk about their less messed up, closer-to-normal life than mine.

I don't know what made me ask him, but I did. "And what about that girl Leah you went with in high school? Leah, right?" He looked at his watch.

"Charlie. Sorry but I gotta head out. Shift starts in an hour."

I wished then that I hadn't opened my stupid mouth. Though why would I be surprised? I hadn't talked to another man other than Jim or his daddy in years. I didn't know how to talk to hardly anybody. Shane asked me to thank Mama and as he headed to his patrol car said, "I'll be by to check in on you again. To make sure you're doing all right." I nodded in slow motion.

None of my life was seeming like it belonged to me, except for the terrible shame and guilt that sat close and that I couldn't shake. Later, when I was telling Shirley about my morning, she would point out to me that when we heard a man and a knock on the door, my first thought hadn't been of Jim. Seeing how that's all my thoughts had been for so long, she said, "You got you a miracle." The tiniest crack of light was squeezing through a lifetime of thick walls I'd built from all the fear and despair I'd been in. "Hope," Shirley said. "And not that fantastical thinking kind you thought was hope when you wanted Jim to welcome you back."

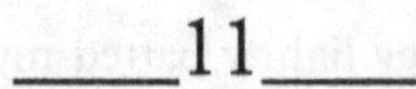

11

"PTSD," Elizabeth Ann said outside the meeting that week. Shirley had picked me up again and Mama had stood out on the porch and waved us off. "That's her hug," I said as Shirley turned on the ignition. Shirley smiled and waved back before shifting up to second. The cab of her truck smelled like cinnamon.

Elizabeth Ann was standing just outside the red, basement door of the church with another woman whose name I couldn't remember, or whether she'd even been there the week before. The lights were on behind them, as well as a light over the door making it harder to see their faces when Shirley and I walked up in the middle of their conversation. Elizabeth Ann seemed less a broken bird as she introduced Jean to me: "This here's Charlie."

Jean nodded at me. She was tall and skinny with short gray hair and wore dark lipstick. I was curious what the color was, thinking it might look good on me, too. I nodded back. They had styrofoam cups in hand and steam was rising into the air mixing with their breath as they talked in the cold. Jean was smoking. "Yes, that's what it is. Fear of the dark, nightmares, flashbacks," she replied.

"Exactly. You know about it, Charlie?" Elizabeth Ann asked, their eyes shifting to look dead at me.

"Umm...yeah. Survivors' group at the hospital. I went once, when I was...well...they talked about it there," I said, my first real sentence uttered to any one of them but Shirley.

"Ahh..." they all three responded as if they remembered hearing it from there, too. That was enough from me.

Jean went on, thank God. "Well, I was on the phone with a young woman I talk to regularly who hasn't slept through the last four nights and is scared she'll never be able to sleep again."

"She'll get tired enough," Shirley added, "and she'll sleep." Jean nodded hard, while the three of them laughed as if it was an odd cooking tip, passed down for generations. Shirley lightly patted my arm as to tell me to keep the tip in mind. Sleep was the one problem I didn't seem to be having, and I wasn't ready to bring up my dreams.

That's when Willow showed up along with Candy, and we all headed inside for the meeting. I ended up next to Willow. She turned to me right off and said, "You look different," then gave me her wide open-mouthed grin, as though she was going to laugh but without sound. I didn't say anything back, but made another note in my mind to ask Shirley what she'd meant on the way home and to add that I was starting to feel different.

I don't know how Willow had gotten all happy with what Shirley said she'd been through and from what later I learned from Willow herself. Turns out she'd had one mean-ass mama, worse than Jim's it sounded like, and then gone and married a man who treated her like a pet rather than a wife. Said she was either a "good dog" or a "bad dog" depending on his mood and seeing how he was a manic depressive, it changed often.

Shirley said that it was the meetings that had turned Willow around. "Much like myself and you, if you keep coming," she said. "What you're seeing in her is gratitude. She's found her identity and support from other women with similar experiences. She and I've talked about it, and she doesn't like to reflect back on what got her here too much, unless she thinks it's gonna help a new person, like you." I was glad as all get-out that Nurse Donna had given me Shirley's phone number. "She'll grow on you, Charlie," Shirley told me with a straight face.

Later, Willow told me in detail the horror she'd witnessed as a child, and her upbeatness did grow on me in time. I got to figuring that us women came in like we were CD's filled with mostly sad or angry songs. Well, Willow had changed hers, filling it with cheesy, happy songs that you can't help but sing along with and laugh at yourself while doing it.

12

"I think it would be good for you to get a job," Mama sprang on me the next day. I hadn't worked in years. In fact, I had maybe worked a total of three months put all together my whole life. I stared at her until she turned back to some sheets she'd been ironing. I grabbed the portable and headed to the porch, cigarette balanced between quivering lips.

I thought about calling Ang, though I hadn't talked to her since the day she told me Jimmy Senior had taken me to the hospital. She had to have been busy being pregnant and all, I told myself. I called Shirley's house. Her husband George answered, "Hold on, Charlie. One sec."

"I hadn't heard horse-shit, nar' a word from the man I'd vowed my life to..." I whined on the phone, telling Shirley what my mama had suggested. "He's supposed to take care of me. Why don't she understand?"

"I think that a job could be of some help to you," Shirley said steady. I couldn't believe those two women would be on the same page. I began to wonder whether Shirley really did know anything about what it was like to walk in my shoes.

Either she was hearing the words I wasn't saying, or else it was the feeble "uh-huhs" I was giving her. "Girl, just for today, look into getting a job. Lots of people have one."

"I don't know."

"It will get you out of your mama's hair for a few hours and give you something to think about that isn't Jim." I hadn't thought about what it was like for Mama to have me back in her house. I never even thought that she might like having some time to herself.

"Try Lenore's Cafe on Main," Shirley added. "Thought I saw a sign up."
I explained that I didn't have much of a resume, hoping she would back off.
"You can use me as a reference. It's Shirley Harris. Can't hurt to try," she
said before hanging up.

§

"Mama? Can I borrow the car?" I asked finding her down the hall in the
living room where her ironing board was set up. As I walked in, she looked
at me suspiciously.

"Mama, can I please borrow the car?"

"What for?"

"A job," I said in a manner that sounded like it wasn't only a handful of
days I had used that same car on my way to commit a felony.

"Well, isn't that something?" she said as she hurried through her last
sweep over an already steamed-flat bedsheet—the same one she'd been
ironing for nearly twenty years. She'd tried to teach me the basics of
housekeeping long before I bled, meaning I's a woman. Ha. Never felt like
one. I took to the mopping, dusting, and ironing. Somehow, I missed the
cooking. I wondered if her training would qualify me for carrying plates to
and from kitchen to table in some restaurant. "I'll come with you," she said.

I got dressed and Mama and I loaded up, me behind the wheel. On our
way we went, driving along Highway 64, fields on our right and mountains
on our left, to get me that job and give her a break from the useless lump
of flesh I'd become.

Lenore's Cafe was on the corner of Main and Broad, in a brick building,
probably as old as the 1800's, across from the courthouse. Mama stayed in
the car as I went inside. It was about thirty minutes before the lunch rush,
so it turned out to be a good a time as any to fill out an application. And it
just so happened that Lenore was available to review it right then and there.

She looked to be Mama's true age, in her fifties or so. Mama looked and acted like she was in her seventies but wasn't. Being married to my daddy must have aged her. Lenore had a gray frosted bob cut above her neckline and mascara like Tammy Faye. She had us sit at one of the tables, me right beside her, my sweaty hands in my lap. She wore black drug-store reading glasses, and the metal chain drooped from the sides as she looked from the paper to my face. "Not much work experience, huh?" she said.

"No ma'am," I replied, sure that was going to be it from me as far as she was concerned. She stared across the room, toward the bar that ran along the backside of the restaurant for over what felt like time passing sitting through one of Pastor Eppleby's sermons. But then she shrugged, folded the application in half, and said plain as a drying wall, "Okay. You got a job." She told me I'd start as a "prep-slash-runner" person while I learned how lunch went. She added that I could start the next day, Wednesday it would be, with the other new girl, Dakota.

I thanked Lenore best I could, but she had moved on away from me to getting the restaurant ready for customers.

"There are no coincidences," Shirley would say when I told her how it'd gone. I was picking up on all kinds of new ideas from that woman. Most I didn't quite get, but she always added the "yet" to any whatever it was, so I didn't worry too much on what I was missing at the time.

"Well, Mama. I got a job," I said scooting into the driver's seat. I can't say I was as thrilled about the new job business, but I was starting to like the idea of getting out of her house.

On the way home, after stopping at the Ingles for some eggs, bacon, and milk, she told me a story that she'd never told me before. When she was first married to my daddy, she didn't think women should work. But they weren't rich folk; Daddy wasn't bringing home enough for Mama to have anything decent with what he was making at Millikan as a low-grade young weave technician. So she took it upon herself to get a job at the local diner. Mama said she didn't ask Daddy because of his stubborn big-headedness, to which she added that that was how you did something you wanted. She said, "You took a risk to do it and told 'im later. Either you got into trouble, or he acted like it was his idea all along."

At that I laughed and Mama took out her hanky from her purse to cover her mouth while she too started to giggle. That made me laugh even more. "Now, now," she said trying to hold respectfully what wasn't supposed to be so funny.

§

I don't know if I saw him before she did, but when we pulled up the drive, his lanky figure was slouched over the railing on the front porch. Mama and I stopped laughing at the same time, as if we'd forgotten how all of a sudden. She barely whispered, "Praise Him," as I put the car in park. Mama hopped out quicker than a jack rabbit, in a hurry to throw her arms around my brother.

Danny looked paler than a newborn's butt and as old as a grandpa. He looked ragged and worn. I knew my prayers right then were different than Mama's. "Dear God," was all I had to offer. I was stuck in the car, too stunned to move. I watched her through the windshield, between mosquito smears, as she reached out to put her hand on his arm and him too ashamed to look at her.

I wondered what he had shown up for. I knew it couldn't be good. I found the strength to get out of the car and walk up the front steps. "I'll get us some lunch," Mama sang and went inside. "Y'all catch up," she added before the screen door eased shut behind her. Was she joking? The boy looked like death had asked to borrow his body. I was scared to know who I was going to be talking to.

I got out my cigarettes and offered him one. He took it without saying anything. I wanted to blurt out, "Just got me a job....First one in forever. Left Jim. Moved back home." But my brother was just staring through me toward the dark tree line, as though there was a view only he could see.

Ten minutes passed with us standing there, smoking our thoughts, our words. "Lunch is ready," Mama hollered from the kitchen. I knew he wasn't going to eat anything but was too scared to call him on it and without the heart to tell her. Her son hadn't really come home, and we'd better hide her checkbook.

Turns out she wasn't going to get more out of him than I did, though she tried. "So, Daniel, this is such a sweet surprise, having you home again," she said, her way of asking him how long he was planning on staying.

"Thanks, Mama," he managed. He took one bite of his ham sandwich but didn't touch his pickle or potato salad, not even a single corn chip. "Well, I wish you'd eat, son," she said with earnest hopefulness in her eyes.

"Aw, well, I ate right before, Mama. Sorry," he replied.

She looked at me. I smiled back at her, working to hide how I thought he was a no-good liar who had come home because he needed something and would break our hearts once again. "Mama, I'm gonna go lay down," he announced, and she told him he could go rest on the sofa, that we'd be quiet, and she'd get him a throw.

The phone rang. I was only too happy to get up from the table to answer it. "Hello?"

"Charlie," said another voice from the dead. "I have to see you," Jim said bluntly as usual but with a distress in his voice that I'd not heard before. Fuck. What was with the day? I carried the portable out to the front porch. I flashbacked to my dream of him in the woods and my head spun as he pleaded with me.

"Now's not a good time, Jim," I heard a me separate from me say.

"What? You're my goddamn wife. Charlie…" I hung up. The phone rang again and then again. That was the beginning of him calling every day.

I dialed Shirley after the 5th time, but George said she was out. I called Willow next. She told me to come right over. I was hesitant to leave Mama alone with Danny, but he was already passed out on the sofa, like he was going to be out for some time. I poked my head in the kitchen to tell her I had taken the phone off the hook. "Who in the world keeps calling, Charlene?" Mama asked.

"It's Jim, Mama."

"Well, you can't talk to him. Doesn't he know that?"

"No, Mama. He doesn't. That's why I took the phone off the hook. All right?"

"I'm not expecting any calls this afternoon."

I told her I needed to step out and see a woman from my group. "Should be just fine," she said. Then she began quietly humming the hymn "Sweet Hour of Prayer" while washing up the dishes from lunch. I decided it was necessary to get my butt to somewhere safe.

§

Willow's house was as I'd always dreamed mine to be. She had the robin's egg blue shutters and even a matching porch swing. I knocked on the door, thinking how normally it was weird going over to someone's house for the first time, but not hers. She answered as her usual, happy self and hugged me like her own child before inviting me in.

She led me straight to her bright, yellow kitchen where she had a large round table surrounded by wooden chairs painted in yellow, red and blue. One was spattered in all three paints. There was a super-sized window over the sink that she'd suctioned hand-painted glass pieces to. On the counter was a collection of juices and glasses, and a steaming teapot on the stove. "What can I get you to drink, dear? You just have a seat now." I sat down in the yellow chair, put my head in my hands and let my tears soak my palms.

"I love him," was all I could say. She handed me some Kleenex and looked at me, her eyes understanding me in that moment like nobody else.

"It isn't easy, Charlie. That's the truth." Through sniffles and near hyperventilation, I told her how I'd met Jim, what it was like when I first saw him and how it felt. She put some hot tea with milk and sugar in front of me, sipped on her own and listened as I went on.

"The other times, well, the first time he raised his hand at me, I was scared. But this last time."

"You were angry," she finished for me.

"I was fucking furious!" I blurted back. "Oh, I'm so sorry," embarrassed for having cussed like that in front of her.

"Of course you were," she agreed waving off my apology.

"What man don't appreciate his wife trying to make him a good meal or at least something homemade?" I asked her. "No-good husband, but God," I kept on, "I wanted him so bad to see me, to appreciate me." I finished and then Willow started telling me about her own life.

Now, I don't really have memories of what my mama went through before my daddy died, though I knew it had been hell for her. But Willow knew clear as a bell as to the suffering caused by her daddy being a cheater and her mama being mean as a snake. I'd never thought a man could go through what we did. Didn't make any sense to me. But Willow said that her daddy crumbled like a child before God in the presence of her mama, Mrs. Danelle Mason.

No matter, because she said, too, that it didn't stop her old man from straying. She said when she was eleven years old, one school night, her daddy was out past his bedtime. Mrs. Mason had taken her pills, mixing them with hard liquor, like usual, as she sat in the kitchen quietly waiting for Willow's daddy to wander home, a chemical storm brewing in her head.

Willow said she was in her room, put to bed in her favorite pink cotton PJs, with her matching robe and slippers hung over a nearby chair. She said her nightlight was plugged in and her door cracked to the hallway. She saw his car lights bounce off her bedroom wall lighting up the shelves he had built, filled with her precious collection of dolls. "About a hundred," Willow said.

She said she remembered the house being so quiet she'd thought her mama had left her there alone. Then she heard the garage door open and close, his car pull in, and her daddy get out and make his way into the house. She heard him stumble down the hall, pause at her door and then proceed to her parents' bedroom. She said then that she couldn't remember how much time had passed before she heard the house filled with a horrific sound, "Like the slaughtering of a pig."

"You can't imagine, Charlie," she said. I couldn't. Willow was telling me one of the worst stories I had ever heard. She was telling it as if she had drifted into some trance above us attached to her words only by a tiny, invisible string.

She said she ran to her parents' room, the door wide open. From the hall light she was able to see her daddy screaming, blood pouring from one eye as her mama stood over him with a screwdriver in her hand.

"It doesn't go away completely," she said to me. "Sometimes I can still hear him."

She said that as she ran to her daddy, her mama sighed, dropped the screwdriver to the floor, wiped her forehead with the back of her hand and walked past little Willow down the hall to the kitchen. Willow said she grabbed the phone next to their bed, called the police by memory not knowing how, and held her daddy in her arms until they arrived, his blood ruining her favorite pink pajamas.

At that, the string that was holding Willow up in her story snapped, and she tumbled back into the kitchen, me staring at her, my mouth wide open. "Honey, you okay? Need more tea?" she said tending back to me.

"I'm so sorry," I managed, wringing my hands.

"My daddy survived but wasn't really the same after. His parents, my grandmother and grandfather, took us in. Of course, my mama went to prison. She died five years back of cancer of the stomach. Was a painful way to die."

I stared at the mug between my hands, my tea barely drank. "One of the times, in the hospital, I had been pregnant," I nearly whispered. "Didn't know until it was too late."

"Oh Charlie. We sure have been through it, haven't we?" I nodded.

"Well, I told you my story so you'd know there's hope. We do heal. In time." I sat there guessing the hope would come once the shame of all I shared had passed.

I thanked her for being so open with me, and that I hated to head on but needed to get back, with my brother being at the house. With that she touched my arm gently, "All right then," she said. "I hope I didn't scare you none."

"I'm terribly sorry you went through what you went through, is all." With that she hugged me at the door. "And thank you for the tea."

"Glad you stopped by, dear. Now we know each other better."

§

When I got home, Danny wasn't asleep on the sofa; he didn't seem to be in the house at all. I peeked in Mama's room, knocking lightly on the door first. She was in a side chair, afghan around her shoulders, working on a new one in rose pink and white. "I'm home," I said

She nodded but didn't look up. "Your brother's gone out."

"When's he comin' back?"

"Don't know. Some boys showed up and he left with 'em," she replied not missing a stitch but her voice trailing. "All I gave him was a twenty. That's all I had in my purse."

I was relieved to hear that. "All right, Mama. I'm heading to bed." It was only a quarter after nine, but I felt as worn as Mama sounded. "I'd better rest up before tomorrow. New job."

"I put the phone back, in case you needed to call home." I had turned to head down the hall and stopped when she said that. "And," she added, "Deputy Perkins called."

I was relieved that Jimmy had given it a rest. And my pulse raced hearing

Deputy Perkins' name.

"Said you didn't need to call him back tonight, the deputy that is, but he may check on you tomorrow after your shift. I told him you'd be starting at Lenore's."

Great. Leave it to Mama to tell him I got a job and where. I really wished I could to talk to Shirley before going to bed but my hand was too heavy to pick up the phone. I was drained from all that I had shared with Willow and all that she'd shared with me. Instead, I washed my face, brushed my teeth, and with what little strength I had, kneeled beside my bed, weighted hands clasped together.

Shirley said it was in the willingness; that it didn't matter what my opinion on the matter was. I gave it a try: "God, grant me the serenity to accept the things I cannot change, the courage to change the things I can, and the wisdom to know the difference. Amen."

I fell asleep so fast that I didn't even hear the door open when Danny came back home.

____13____

I awoke before my alarm went off, with a clear vision of another dream I had just had. What I didn't have, though, was a clear idea of what it meant.

In the dream I had been in a stranger's room, which had two fireplaces, both cold, a bed, and lots of brown everywhere: brown curtains, brown bedspread, brown pillows, brown-beige walls. Like the pigskin of a football brown, and all over. The only thing that had color was a tiny picture in a white square frame of a little girl with blond hair and a huge grin on her face. She had butterfly wings for arms that were all the colors of the rainbow. It was as if she was flying through the sky as the clouds blew past her. The picture hung over the left of the two fireplaces.

Next, my brother walked in with two other guys I'd never seen before. They looked tough, as if they'd traveled the back roads burning fields of grass in their wake.

"Jesus, Danny," I said. "What are you doing with them?"

He didn't look as mean as them, nor did he have that pale and deathly face he had standing on Mama's porch the day before. "We can't sleep, Charlie, with that pilot light going like that," he said.

"What was he talking about?" I wondered. I went over to the fireplaces to show him how ridiculous he was and saw a small light from under the plastic wood. I was annoyed with him for pointing it out to me.

I would have to try, but as I went to turn the flame down, the smaller of the fireplaces—the one facing the bed—ignited the wood inside. I thought, "Oh now look what I've done."

My alarm finally went off. I laid there, covers thrown back to my feet, my body toasty, and wondered what Shirley would have to say about those dreams. I was going to have to tell her about them, since they didn't seem to be going away. I replayed the details a good ten minutes, hoping to remember, and thanked God Jim wasn't in that one. It seemed the more I was surrendering my waking life, the crazier my dreams got, as if they were sorting through the riffraff, like cleaning out a cluttered closet.

§

I got to Lenore's before Dakota, the other new girl, had arrived so Lenore had me sit at a table and wait while she and one of the other waitresses got busy opening up the register and brewing coffee. I had already had enough myself at the house to jumpstart a lawnmower, so I sat there, my nerves like bouncing beans, wondering when we'd get smoke breaks. I was relieved to learn I could step out the side door anytime and squeeze one in.

Before I had time to wander off in my head with all my worries, a tall redhead walked in, hips narrower than one of my thighs. She apologized for being late. She stuck her arm out to me, a grin on her face, and I could see she had a little gap between her two front teeth. "Hey. I'm Dakota," she said in a worse drawl than mine.

"I'm Charlie," I said, before Lenore stepped over with another waitress following her.

"All right, girls, this here's Sandy. She's gonna show you how to prep." To Sandy and Sandy's unimpressed expression, she said, "Get them girls some shirts and an apron."

Dakota and I followed Sandy back to a closet by the bathroom, mouths shut. She pulled a box down from the top shelf and pulled out our uniforms, which was one navy shirt with Lenore's name on it in gold thread and one brown apron. Looked like we were going to have to wash our one and only shirt every day when Sandy informed us that we'd be buying a second one once we made some money. Dakota seemed to want to say something, pulling in her breath, but since Sandy hadn't appeared the least bit interested in us, she turned to biting her nails.

I went to the bathroom and put my shirt on. The damn thing felt tighter than I'd have liked, but Dakota nodded her approval when I came out. Since she was a pencil, hers was a bit baggy. God, grant me a cigarette.

Our first lesson was in making the tea. Sandy showed us where the restaurant-size tea bags and the sugar bin were and how much to use before hitting the brew button. Dakota didn't look to be paying attention. She stared out past Sandy's head when she talked, but then Sandy moved fast like a flea, so it was hard to keep track.

Next she led us to where the salt and pepper refills were and handed us a tray and a rag each. "Go around to all the tables and fill them up." We did that, me getting to way more than Dakota.

After that was the ketchup. Then the cracker baskets. I got the sense that I was going to be doing most of the work, unless Dakota was having a one-off lazy first day.

Once we were done with the floor, Sandy took us to the salad station. We checked to see how much was left over from the day before and headed behind the kitchen, past the sink and dish racks to the cooler. Sandy went in first, handing to Dakota who then handed to me, heads of lettuce, tomatoes, cucumbers, and carrots.

Sandy gave us the basic run-down for chopping the veggies. As I got started, Dakota did, too, though much slower, like she had been struck with mono. That's when she started talking. "Funny I'd never seen you before. Guess we went to different schools. Parents worked at Smith and Brown on the other side of the mountain."

All Dakota needed from me was an "uh-huh" here and there, and she was good to keep going. "I never been married, you?" I chopped about three times the speed she did. I was wondering how we were going to fare as waitresses, what with me being shy and her being a sorry worker.

I didn't feel like sharing my story: a) while on the job day one and b) with a girl I barely knew twenty minutes. She didn't wait for me to answer. "I've been dating this guy Cole. Not much of a romantic. Loves hunting and drinking. Ain't no crazy surprise, you know. Sometimes he's so sweet, makes me cry. Started living together a few months back." I'm not sure what she wanted me to say, so I nodded and kept chopping.

Sandy came back to check on us and started pulling out plastic plates for salads. "Make about fifty," she said as she demonstrated the amount of lettuce, number of carrots, slices of tomatoes, and croutons per plate. She pointed to the trays we'd use to keep them on and the cooler by the service station where they'd be kept to chill during lunch.

"I don't care that he drinks a bit much," Dakota continued once Sandy left. Then she switched to me, "Hey, you ever go outta town? Like to the beach?"

"No," I replied plainly.

"Oh, girl, we gotta get you to the beach once the weather gets warm. You look like you could use some sun," she said as if she weren't herself a redhead, pale as bone china with speckled flakes in it. I laughed to myself.

She went on. "I love the ocean. I have to be careful with my skin, is all. Just makes my freckles stand out more. Before Cole there was this guy Darrel Miller, you know 'im?"

"Nah."

"Darrel was a decent enough guy. He took me to the beach for my birthday which is in late June. Makes me a Cancer. Lord, was it hot. The ocean felt like bath water."

"Wait," I said, pausing at a carrot. "You have cancer?"

"What? Oh no! Why would you?"

"You said, 'Makes me a...'"

"Astrology! I'm a Cancer. You don't know of astrology?"

My face flushed red. I went back to the carrot. Dakota continued. She told me her Aunt Rosaline had been her mama's sister and practically disowned her mama because she'd gotten into astrology. Dakota said that Aunt Rosaline told her mama she was working for the Devil and teaching her daughter the evil ways and she wouldn't have nothing to do with it. They didn't talk for years. Aunt Rosaline sounded like my mama.

Dakota went on. "Then Aunt Rosaline ended up getting actual cancer and my mama was the one to go take care of her. She was there with her when she took her last breath. Mama said they prayed together right before. Lord's Prayer. And that her sister told her then that she knew she wasn't of the Devil and to forgive her for judging her so."

"I've heard of astrology, by the way," I said. But her talking about the beach, well, our family didn't take trips. We didn't "vacation." The outskirts of Eden's Gap was as far as I'd ever been.

The more plates we made, I realized that I'd be doing prep work like we were doing over and over every day of the week for weeks on end, maybe years. I'd daydreamed of being a good Southern cook for my husband, but that was one person. We were putting together food for nearly fifty people, and the repetition was getting right out boring. And it was only my first day.

"Darrel Miller and I made out in the water, waves picking me up off my feet," Dakota continued. "Even went out at night. Was a bit creepy. Kept thinking everything that brushed my leg was gonna take a bite."

And then she laughed. It was such a loud "ha" that I came close to dumping the crouton container full to the floor. Sandy walked back to check on us and grabbed one of the trays, rearranging some of the plates so they'd balance better as she walked. "Lunch starts in about ten minutes," she said as she rounded the corner back to the floor.

A young guy, dirty blond, had come in the back door while Dakota was blabbing on and on, followed by a stocky brown-haired woman. They had on funky patterned pants that looked like parachute pants from high school, a fad that came late and didn't last at my school. The brown-haired woman had a husky voice, and she and the guy were talking smack to each other, like guys do. They didn't pay us a lick of attention.

I finished the rest of the salad plates when the brown-haired lady started barking at Dakota, "Hey. You. New chick. Come here." With a look of surprise, Dakota went over to the cook's station. "Pull me out some tomatoes and mayo from the cooler, will you?" she bossed. At least Dakota wasn't dumb enough to think she had an option.

Sandy pulled me out to the front. "If you wanna smoke, now's the time to do it, but you gotta do it out there," and she pointed to the side door by the shelves where we kept our purses to the outside where she was headed. I got my pack and lighter from mine stuffed on top of old menus and followed her out in silence.

Sandy's face had a faded, gray look, but I was guessing she wasn't but five years older than me. "Maryl and Ty are the cooks. Don't get in their way," she warned. It was too late for Dakota, who hadn't had a chance. Her being as tall as she was with that flamed hair didn't help her hide much.

"They will take time to get used to," Sandy added. You should meet Jim, I wanted to say.

Ty stepped out and snarled, "Who are you?"

"That's Charlie," Sandy answered for me.

"Ty," he said as he stuck his hand out for me to shake. I reached my hand out, and with that he pulled his hand away, laughing at me as he headed back inside. I looked down at a large crack in the sidewalk wishing

I was back at Mama's, the idea of this job thing having already turned against me.

"Like I said," Sandy said as she went in behind him. I followed her wishing the day would get along already.

Dakota was by the bar at the front of the restaurant. Lenore was going over tickets with her. She called me over for last minute instructions, which consisted of staying out of the cooks' way and the wait staff's way and to be ready to get them whatever they needed as quickly as possible. Oh, and we'd be helping to bus tables, clearing plates and empty glasses.

Another waitress came in. Her name was Ida. She looked too fragile to be lifting the trays I saw Sandy lift with one hand. She seemed the most friendly, giving us a real smile before going to the back to get her apron and tickets ready.

I didn't know what to expect, but I sure wasn't ready for the onslaught of people that came through that place from noon to 1:30. My feet hurt as I ran around like a chicken with its head cut off.

After the rush, about two or three tables lingered. "Halfbacks," Dakota whispered picking up a few of the cracker baskets from empty tables. Being a mountain town, we had our fair share of retired Yankees who lived part-time in Florida and part-time in Eden's Gap. I had never heard a term for them, but I hadn't been out in the town since I had been married and had missed the goings on.

Since Sandy had come in first, she got to batch out early. I was wiped out, and we still had sweeping and mopping to do. Even Dakota had run out of juice; she hadn't said much in the last fifteen minutes.

"Good job, girls," Lenore praised when we finished up. She told us we'd get minimum wage while we stayed as prep help and checks were every two weeks. I filled a big styrofoam cup, emptying the last of the sweet tea. I hoped Mama had something for me at home to eat, though. I was starving.

Dakota and I walked out together. "Where'd you park?" she asked.

"Around back. You?"

"Same."

I lit a cigarette and offered her one. "No, thanks."

"How come? You don't smoke?"

"Mama has emphysema," she replied. "You heard of it?"

"Is that a lung thing?"

"Yep. A lung disease. Lots of mucus and coughing. Lungs get worse over time. She's been on oxygen for the last two years. Carries a tank around wherever she goes."

"That's a shame," I said, sorry for her mama's condition. I kept to myself how I couldn't imagine not smoking.

"Whatcha doing later?" she asked, unable to walk in silence.

"Just going home."

"Oh. And where's that?"

Her getting into my business was not what I was in the mood for. I rathered her going back to talking about herself. "Up Still Woods Road," I answered anyway. "Not too far off Pickett's Highway." There was no way I was going to add that I had left my no-good husband and was living with my mama again. I had taken my ring off right after I'd gone to find Jim with his own pistol.

Dakota didn't press. Getting into her rusty red Ford Escort, she shouted, "Nice to meet you, Charlie!" I nodded and smiled. As I was getting in my car, she rolled down her window and called out, "When's your birthday?"

"What?" I yelled back not sure I heard her.

"I said, 'When's your birthday?'" she shouted loud enough for folks across the street to hear.

Puzzled I yelled back, "March 11th!"

"You're a Pisces!" she exclaimed, thrilled by the news. "We're compatible, you and me!" Then she waved good-bye and backed her car up, grinning her gapped smile at me, and drove off. Astrology seemed like a big deal to Dakota, where I'd barely given it much of a wandering thought.

§

Danny was on the porch smoking when I got home. He looked like a coat rack, skinny as he was, standing there in an old winter jacket he'd had from high school. I didn't know what he could have been doing all day, but I hoped to God he wasn't robbing Mama blind, not that she had much. What little jewelry she had and the glassware she'd collected over the years wasn't worth anything but the meaning it had to her.

He didn't say hello when I walked past to go inside. Neither did I. It was Thursday, and I was going to need a quick nap before my meeting. First though, I had to grab a snack.

Mama was in the kitchen making a grocery list. It smelled like Pine Sol, as if she'd washed the floor not long before I got home. She stopped when I walked in and told me to sit so she could fix me a sandwich. I pulled out the chair next to her. "Ham, lettuce, and mayo then," she let me know before getting up to make it.

"How was your first day?" she asked, a dim halo of light around her poofy hair as she stood at the counter layering mayonaise on two pieces of Wonderbread.

"It was all right," I answered.

"Well, the Lord sure is good, bringing you a chance to serve Him in the community." She handed me my sandwich, then sat back down and clasped her hands. "Let us give thanks." I clasped my hands, as well. "Amen." I wolfed down my sandwich within minutes, excused myself, asking her to make sure I was up by no later than four-thirty and thanking her.

"Praise Him," I thought I heard Mama say from down the hall as I closed the door to my room.

§

When Shirley picked me up, she had on a new wrap, this one multicolored but mostly a firey red. The truck cab smelled like orange and spice. "Oh my God, am I tired," I complained. My nap did little and my feet were aching. Mama had said I needed to soak them in Epsom salts. Shirley agreed. She pulled out onto the mountain highway into town. The sun was setting just off to our left, rays of sun and half-globes of pinks and blues in our eyes.

"You know Lenore runs a shelter for women?" Shirley asked.

"What for?"

88

"For battered women, Charlie. Like we were."

"And she runs that restaurant, too?" I asked. I couldn't think how she could manage both.

"Yep, she's had some real tragedy in her life."

"What happened?" I asked coming to think we all have us some tragedy.

"About 10 years ago, Lenore's daughter was killed by her husband."

"Jesus," I whispered. Chill bumps ran up my arms. I should stop complaining about my feet. At that I confessed, "Jim's been calling."

"You talking to him?" she asked sounding concerned.

"Nah. Well, once. Yesterday. I told him I had to go. And he kept calling, but I took the phone off the hook." Shirley was silent for a minute. We turned down Main Street. "That's why I called you."

"Well, I'm sorry I wasn't available, dear," she said and I knew she meant it.

"It's all right. I went to Willow's," I told her and relayed my time with Willow in the few minutes I had before we reached the church.

"I know her story well," Shirley said. "I'm glad she shared it with you so you could know her better. It's a miracle we're still here, hon. Isn't it?" She wasn't expecting me to answer, I could tell. Just then, Willow pulled up behind us in the parking lot, waving as usual with a wide smile on her face.

In the meeting, I had Willow on my left and Shirley on my right. There were only six of us there that night, with Elizabeth Ann, Jean, and Candy being the other three. I guess a third meeting is a charm, because I told the group just about everything: about my new job, about Danny being home, and about Jim calling. I told them that I was tired from working and tired from the worry.

Willow shared about how happy she was to have so many great women in her life. She shifted her smile to Candy, adding a nod, then a light pat on Candy's shoulder. Candy kept her eyes on her hands, her fingers folded tightly. "I'll pass," she whispered, a piece of her blond and stringy hair falling across her face.

It was Elizabeth Ann's turn, and she shared about her volunteer work at a community program for families doing bookkeeping and light accounting. She said how having something that got her out of her house helped her.

The other woman, Jean, with her scratchy voice, deep like a man's, shared about her nephew who was just turning forty and who was struggling with drugs. She said he was coming to live with her after getting out of treatment. Turns out Jean had been a nurse at Mission's Baptist Hospital up near Henderson, a forty-five minute drive north of Eden's Gap, for nearly twenty years. She was the last to talk, and we stood to hold hands before ending the meeting. I knew I was lucky to be standing there.

Leaving the meeting, Jean told me that she thought my exhaustion was a good thing early on and that if you had a good night's sleep, count that as a blessing. She was right: I'd had no problems sleeping, and I wasn't having any nightmares.

I was seeing how women you wouldn't expect to become friends did, from going through what we had, like Elizabeth Ann and Jean. The two of them were still talking outside after Shirley and I said our goodbyes and got in her truck. As Shirley pulled out of the parking lot, I thought next time I'd ask Jean if she knew Nurse Donna, even though they worked at two different hospitals.

On the ride home, I brought up my dreams. "That's your subconscious doing some housecleaning," she told me as the trees whirred by. It was dark, without much of a moon to light the sky. "Sounds like you're ready to start some spiritual work."

I'd heard the word "subconscious" before, but I didn't know how it related to me and wasn't sure what she had in mind that she was calling "spiritual work." I was doubting I could handle something new, what with starting my new job and all. I stared ahead, watching the twisting and turning of the road before us. "It's necessary that we do this so we don't go back," she continued. "We have to come to terms with our obsessive natures—our need for others to make us feel right about ourselves."

"Sure. I understand," I said, even though I didn't. She eyed me quickly, and I knew she knew goddamn well I wasn't buying it.

"Doing this 'work' will help it make more sense," she said. "And in case you don't know, our subconscious is our ideas of life that are buried inside us. They can reveal themselves to us sometimes in dreams and in doing what I'm going to share with you."

We were nearly to Mama's when she gave me her instructions on reading and writing about myself—starting my life history. She called it Step One. Shirley said that the women's group used the Twelve Steps like in Alcoholics Anonymous and Al-Anon in order to work on themselves. I'd heard of AA but didn't know anything about it or anybody who went and the word "Al-Anon" sounded like she'd made it up.

"Well, okay," was all I had to say.

"They're just guidelines. Tools. Amazing tools." She about glowed when she talked about all this stuff. She also said to continue the morning routine, which was the prayer, silent time, and journaling.

"And my dreams? Do I do anything about them?" I asked.

"Definitely write those down," she directed, adding, "They are important, and the more aware you become of what's going on with you in your waking life, the more relevant your dreams will be to you."

Luckily at that, we headed up the gravel drive to the house. She'd given me a lot to think about, and it seemed a bit much all at once. I was glad to say goodnight. Mama had left the porch light on for me. I wondered if I needed to leave it on for my brother yet.

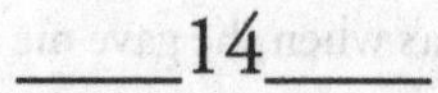

14

My schedule at Lenore's was that I worked four days a week: Tuesday, Wednesday, Thursday, and Saturday. Dakota and I were now waiting tables with either Sandy or Ida. I was so drained from work most days I was fairly useless at home, including doing any of the new "spiritual work" for Shirley.

Jim was still calling every day. Shirley said that talking to him wouldn't help him or me (me being who she cared about). She'd say that he was just lonely, as he should be. I took her advice about not talking to him but couldn't seem to part with my wedding ring, as rinky-dink as it was. I'd taken it off my hand but kept it in view on my nightstand. I didn't have the strength, or courage, to think about my future without him.

§

Danny had taken off again that next Tuesday, which didn't surprise me any. He had left and hadn't come back that night or the next day. Even though Mama was happy when he first arrived, she seemed to relax more once he had gone again. She and I fell into a routine with each other. The house was quiet and Christmas was coming. Mama wanted me to go to church with her on Sundays. I agreed even though I didn't really want to.

I hadn't heard hide nor hair of Deputy Shane for weeks, until he showed up at Lenore's the Saturday after Thanksgiving. He'd come in with a girl I didn't recognize. I avoided looking in his direction best I could. After the rush while we were in back cleaning up Dakota asked, "Who's that man who keeps looking at you and whose table you won't go near?" He had been there for over an hour. Lunch shouldn't take that long, I thought.

"Went to high school with him," I replied, not giving her the answer she was fishing for. I had noticed him looking at me, too, but I didn't think it did me any good to get excited when he was occupied with someone else. And she was attractive, the girl he'd brought in. She looked skinny, the slender kind and had a short, brown bob showing off her long neck. Before Dakota would try to get more out of me, I grabbed my smokes from my purse and turned to go out the side door. Shane stood in front of me as he had come to the back to wait for the bathroom, his broad shoulders square to me. He wore a plaid flannel shirt tucked into dark jeans. He smelled of aftershave, clean.

"Hey, Charlie."

"Hey," I said a bit startled and annoyed and happy to talk to him.

"You doing okay?"

"Sure." I looked back towards the dining room where his lady friend sat, eyes darting from the table toward the bathrooms.

"I forgot that you worked here," he said. In a way, it was as if he was apologizing for being here with her. It wasn't like he owed me anything. He wasn't mine.

"Yep," I said, short-like. I could see his date staring at us, me in particular, as if she had anything to worry about.

"I should get my smoke in," I said finally. I didn't know how to stand there with him acting like he'd hurt me somehow. We'd never been out. Yes, he had saved my life. It wasn't romantic. "It was his job," I told myself. But I couldn't help but feel out-of-sorts that he'd stopped calling and then shown up where I worked with another woman.

He touched my arm and said gently, "Take care. You're looking more like the Charlie I remembered."

"Well, that's a relief," I thought. I had the husband I wanted but couldn't be with calling and the honorable and kind man who I didn't know I wanted but did, seeing someone else. For the first time since living in the trailer I thought about getting high.

§

When I finally got to the quiet of my car after my shift, I bawled my eyes out. I was going to head home but ended up taking a detour down the mountain, past the tire place, and on through Redman. I kept driving, crossing the state line, and stopped for a Coke and a Snickers at a gas station off Highway 17. I made eye contact with some biker fellow, probably coming from Tank's place high on God knows what. I hadn't thought about sex in a while, but he called me over to his bike and asked if I wanted to go for a short ride. It wasn't dark yet. I didn't know him, but "fuck it" was the mood I was in.

His name was Rick. His short hair was tucked under a blue bandana. He said we'd head toward Trout Lake, not more than five miles east. Sure, I was in. I hopped on, grabbing ahold of his jacket and knowing I'd be freezing as soon as we set off. He revved up his Fat Boy and I felt a rush— but it lasted less than a minute.

I rested my chin on his shoulder, his leather vest hard underneath, the wind burning my eyeballs and blowing dry the tears spilling down my cheeks. Rick stopped on the side of the road and lit a joint. I took a hit, welcoming the sweetness and letting the pain in my head go. He led me into the woods and started kissing my neck. I let him lay me down on a patch of pine needles and unbutton my pants. We fucked quickly before hopping on his bike to head back. It was dark then, and I had lost the feeling in my fingers, toes, and other parts.

I drove back up the mountain in a haze full of nothing and luckily I never crossed the yellow line or hit a tree before pulling into Mama's drive.

"Danny's in jail," Mama said as soon as I walked in the house. She came out of the living room on her way to the kitchen. I was hoping she'd be out. I went straight to the bathroom. "Deputy Shane called to let me know." Great, I thought. I was high and was going to have to deal with Deputy Shane again.

"Leave 'im," I huffed, looking into the bathroom mirror to see how bloodshot my eyes were. I splashed my face with cold water and stared at my reflection. My eyes were red and puffy. I looked like I felt: defeated.

I hesitantly went to the kitchen, needing a snack.

"We'll go down to the Police station tomorrow after church," Mama said, as she was folding up the minty green table cloth she had been ironing. Had been her mama's. We rarely ate on it, but she would hand wash it, iron, fold and put it away from time-to-time to keep it fresh.

"Do him some good being locked up over night." I opened the fridge to get out the milk.

"Hopefully," she replied. "I invited Deputy Shane to supper."

"Tonight?" I about shrieked. I half turned to her, because I still didn't want her to know that I had gotten high.

"Charlene Louise. What has gotten into you?" She stood across from the ironing board, holding two corners of the sheet in mid air. "Not tonight. Sunday. One Sunday before Christmas."

"Mama," I managed much calmer, "Did he say why Danny's in jail?"

"Bad folks he's running with."

"But what'd Shane say, Mama?" On the counter next to the fridge was the red and white tin that Mama filled with her homemade cookies most weeks. I opened it to find walnut and chocolate chip. The smell of brown sugar and butter rose up, and I got out a plate to put them on. Then I poured myself a glass of milk.

"You're gonna ruin your dinner."

"I ate," I lied. "Plus, I'm only having a few." Another lie.

"Said he robbed a convenience store. That's what Deputy Shane said."

It was as if she wasn't believing it. I knew she thought he was innocent somehow.

"That's a big deal, Mama."

"Just pray for him, Charlie. Let's let the Lord take care of this."

I took a plate of cookies and my milk to go watch some TV in the back room. It had been a porch a ways back. Danny had closed it off and moved Daddy's recliner out there. There was only a space heater, so it never got too warm. Mama never upgraded it because she never watched TV and had no interest sitting in Daddy's recliner, even though she'd never get rid of it either. I grabbed an afghan from the living room and cranked up the heater hot as it could go. I fell asleep to a rerun of "Smokey and The Bandit" and then awoke weak and dehydrated. I guzzled water from the bathroom faucet, then flopped myself into bed.

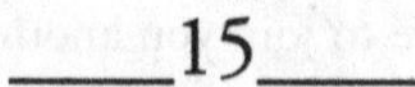

15

Mama came into my room at seven the next morning, waking me in time to get ready for church. I had a terrible thirst, my mouth feeling like a wad of cotton balls. I found some BC Powder in the medicine cabinet, turned on the faucet, and gulped straight from the sink again.

"I called the police station this morning," she told me on the way to church. "A nice young lady answered. She told me Danny was all right." I wasn't so sure about that, I thought to myself. As long as Mama got comfort from thinking that way, well, I would go along with it.

The front pillars of the church had berry-red ribbon wrapping on them and wreaths with matching bows hung on the front doors. We entered through the back and up the basement stairs. It gave Mama some pride being as involved as she was, like the church was her house and she was coming from her own kitchen to greet her guests.

Of all the church ladies, Nadene was Mama's oldest friend. She was almost eighty but loved Mama like a sister. The two of them acted like they ran the place.

"Good to see you, dear," Nadene said to me, squeezing my arm with a pale, wrinkled hand. I did my best to smile and not seem too hung over, though I'm not sure how they didn't see that my eyes practically matched the decorations. Mama greeted Pastor Eppleby next and up we went to sit for the next hour and a half. The sermon was the buildup to Jesus being born. Nearing Christmas, Pastor Eppleby was overly excited and even longer winded than usual.

After what seemed like an eternity, the narrow pew cushion not doing much to soften my seat, he wrapped it up. At the end of service, Nadene turned to us and asked, "Why don't you join us at Monroe's?" Her husband stood beside her, equally old and wrinkled and not appearing interested in whether we were coming to Sunday Dinner or not.

"Awfully kind. We'll have to join you another day," Mama replied. We had somewhere else to be she wasn't going to mention, not even to her closest friend.

We said our goodbyes and then I drove us to the police station that sat in the middle of town. It was blocks away from Lenore's. I knew Mama was praying that nobody would see her car parked in back. Of course, if anybody read the paper, they'd find out.

I followed Mama, her head up, as she marched inside as if we were walking into LuLu's Flower Shop picking up a birthday bouquet instead of the police station to visit my meth-head, gone-gotten-himself-arrested brother.

"We're here to see Daniel Alan Montgomery," Mama said in the same manner she'd walked in with.

"Didn't I speak to you on the phone early this morning?" asked the receptionist.

"Yes. Yes, we spoke," replied Mama.

I stood beside her like a useless dope. I was worried about her seeing Danny; I knew he wasn't going to look so good. "Is Deputy Perkins here?" Mama asked next. I froze.

"He is. I can call him out front, if you like."

"Mama...No."

She ignored me. "That would be fine. Thank you."

Great. Now he was going to get to deal with the whole of us, me and Danny, all a complete mess, as we were. Shane came out quickly as if he'd been expecting us. "Hi there, Mrs. Montgomery. Charlie." He greeted us kindly, considering the circumstances. "Follow me."

We went with him past a few offices and through a door that he had to type numbers into a lock pad to open. There weren't but a few cells, more like small rooms. Danny was in the one at the end. "He can't go home with you today," Shane informed us before letting us in. Mama looked back at me. "Thank you," I replied for both of us.

Danny was sitting on a cot. He had on an issued jumpsuit and his hair was long and greasy. Mama took out her hanky and held it to her nose. The boy flat out stank like he had been sitting in his own piss for days on end. I didn't know what we were supposed to say to him. Deputy Shane stood outside the door while Mama sat down beside him on the cot.

"We can't take you home today, son," she said as if she was repeating the deputy's words to herself, for her sake more than Danny's. I was shaking and wanted to smoke; Mama looked calm and determined. "But we'll be taking you home soon enough, you hear me?"

Danny stared down at his feet in the slippers they'd given him. "You hear me, Daniel?" she repeated, even more firm-like, as if she was now telling God that she would be taking her son home, end of story. But Danny didn't nod his head or even blink his eyes to indicate he'd heard her. She patted his hand and we were done.

"Now Mrs. Montgomery, this could be a drawn-out process," Shane was telling her, as he escorted us back to the front of the station. We stood a moment in the open area where we had come in, the sign on the glass, EDEN'S GAP POLICE STATION, behind Mama's small body, stamping into time us being there. Her simple, maroon dress, her navy handbag, her eyes looking up at the Deputy.

Shane shifted weight. "Danny will be here for up to 48 hours and then they'll move him to County. He will meet with a defense attorney, an appointed one, before his initial court hearing. Or you can hire one. But more likely than not, given the nature of the arrest, his bail will be high.

Really high."

Mama clasped her purse, as if she was going to open it and grab her check book. "Mrs. Montgomery, he won't get out before his hearing."

"Good," I thought to myself. "Will do him good stayin' in there as long as they can keep him."

"Mama," I said, "Do you understand what Deputy Shane is saying?" She looked at me and then looked at him.

"We won't be taking any more of your time, Son. You've been so kind. Now, we are looking forward to having you over for supper soon." And like that, she turned facing the door until Deputy Shane opened it for her to let her out. He put his hand on my shoulder giving it a light squeeze, as I trailed Mama out the door. "Let me know if there's anything you need," he said.

"Sure. Thanks," I replied hoping that he wasn't able to tell how much my body temperature went up when he touched me.

On the drive home, I was thinking about when I'd see Shane again. Was he really coming to eat with us the next week? I stopped myself before I laughed out loud. "If old habits don't die a painful, slow death," I thought. "If it ain't one fella, it's another."

"We'll need to hire us a lawyer," Mama said, reminding me why we had been at the police station to begin with. The day was cold and bleak. The clouds overhead were heavy.

"Yep, Mama, that's what Shane was saying would be a good idea."

It dawned on me then that I could be there for my mama, more sober than not. She wasn't going to have to deal with my brother's troubles alone. The day before, hooking up with that biker guy seemed like a glitch, a hiccup. That was not the woman I wanted to be anymore. The desire to escape, lifting.

There were three messages on the answering machine when we got in, all from Jim. Lord, what had gotten into that man? He sounded sweet and nothing like the man I'd been married to. I called Shirley. She was out, so

I left a message with George. Then I called Willow. I was torn, the idea of leaving Mama alone once more given the circumstances, but I needed to talk with one of the women from my group. Jim's messages were working themselves over on me.

"Come, come, sweetie," Willow chirped. At that, I couldn't wait to step onto her porch and see her smiling face.

"Looks like we may get snow," Mama said from the kitchen with the radio turned on. It was always set to the local religious station, WRHC, out of Henderson.

"I'll be back before dark," I told her.

"You're not going to eat first?"

"Naw, Mama. Gonna visit my friend Willow."

"Be careful driving."

Guilt sneaks in many doors, and me heading out leaving her there after just coming from seeing Danny like he was, the guilt was pushing it's way in. But I had to leave for the moment. I would be back soon, I told myself. I grabbed the keys and gave her a kiss on the cheek before practically running out the door. When I looked back she was pulling cold cuts from the fridge.

"So, I think I have a crush on this guy," I said as Willow handed me a plate of her special grilled cheese sandwich and a cup of tomato soup.

"Wow, that's good," I said wiping melted cheddar from my lip with the paper napkin she'd handed me.

"Thank you, darling. The secret is mayonnaise. Now, what about this crush?"

I told her about Deputy Shane and my moment of desperation that I'd had with the gun going after Jim. And then I told her about Shane saying he would check on me after and how he never did, but then showed up a month later at the restaurant with that burrowing-eyed woman.

"Dang, Charlie."

"I know, right? I didn't know I even cared 'til I saw him with her."

"That'll do it. Seein' 'im with another woman."

"So then here's what I did...." And I told her about driving down the mountain, about not thinking twice and getting high with that Rick guy, then having sex with him, a stranger in the woods.

As soon as I took a breath, she asked, "You tell Shirley, yet?"

"Not yet," I admitted.

"Might be good to do so." I told her I would. Willow listened to me go on and on talking about the day's events including seeing my brother in jail. Finishing with Danny, I went right back to talking about Shane.

"I wanna tell him," I said feeling the urgency.

"Tell him what?" she asked.

"That I like him."

She replied with a "hmmm" and then asked me if I wanted some tea as she stood up to put a pot of water on the stove.

"My advice?" she asked. I nodded.

"Be patient," she said. I moaned. "I know it's hard. But a man's gotta be a man. They like to make the first move. You gotta let him. You start doing for him what he's supposed to do and you'll be doing it forever—that is, if it's meant to be."

I added sugar and milk to the tea she'd put in front of me. There was a knock at the front door and then we heard, "Hello?" I looked up to see Shirley walking into the kitchen.

"So, weather looks like snow to me!" she said wearing a bright red lipstick. It matched the scarf she had on: woven red, purple, and green with long fringe on the ends.

"Love this," Willow said running her fingers through the fringe.

"Gift to myself," Shirley replied. "Christmas shopping for the family and cannot seem to stop myself. Hi, dear," she said to me, leaning over to hug my neck. She smelled of incense, like her truck. All the open affection was new to me. It was unusual but felt good, like welcoming rain after a long draught.

"I left a message for you," I said to her.

"Well, I'm answering," she teased. Willow grabbed another mug for Shirley and before the snow started to come down, the three of us sat in Willow's kitchen and told crazy old husband stories. As sad as our stories were, we laughed our tails off. I would never have thought that women like Willow and Shirley could be so funny.

"I'd better get back to Mama," I said after a while and got up to leave.

"So glad you dropped in," Willow said as I headed out the door.

"We'll talk tomorrow," said Shirley, giving me no reason to believe otherwise.

§

"When's his birthday?" Dakota asked after our shift that following Friday. She was asking me about Deputy Shane, since I had somehow started opening up to her in a way that was as uncommon for me, but becoming more so, as planting a kiss on my mama's cheek or letting Shirley hug my neck.

"I have no idea." We stood by our cars in the back lot. I had a large sweet tea in one hand and a cigarette in the other, my fingers white on the tips from standing in the cold. The snow that had come and went all week was in dirty piles along the curb and the ground was slushy. I could see Dakota's breath as she talked.

"Well, you can tell a lot about a person from their birthday. But we'd also need his exact time of birth."

"Hmm…" I was trying to figure out how I'd possibly get that information without him thinking me nuts. But then I didn't know how much crazier a person could seem after being pulled over with a gun in the passenger seat on their way to kill their husband and his lover only to be followed up by meeting them and their mama at the jailhouse visiting their son/brother for armed robbery. "Getting an exact time of birth might be the sanest thing he's known me to do," I thought.

"So, are you getting a divorce?" Dakota asked. I stared blankly back at her. She crossed her arms. "Well, I'd love to see Shane's chart, but we've got nothing to work with," she explained, as if that was her excuse for getting further into my business, which I wasn't inviting her into.

She looked back at me, quiet, with her red hair tucked up in an olive green, knitted hat. Her being so tall, looming above a moment, I felt pressure to know, to have an answer. But I didn't have one. I took a hit off my cigarette and told her I had to get home.

"Divorce ain't easy!" she called out as I got in the car.

§

One of the biggest miracles within the last several months was that I hadn't run into Jim anywhere. It could be that I didn't go to bars, and he was always in them. I didn't ever go near the tire shop, except the other day driving past on the way down the mountain. He never came by Mama's, either. I'm guessing he was scared Mama knew how to use Daddy's old shotgun, and it'd be risky showing up without an invitation.

He'd been leaving messages nonstop, but with Shirley's guidance, I didn't call him back. Unfortunately, that afternoon, I answered the phone without thinking, and lo and behold, he was on the other end. "I need to see you," he cooed at me.

"It ain't happening."

"Baby, you don't understand. You're my wife."

He had a point. I was.

When I got off the phone with Jim I was rattled. I wiped my hands on my jeans. Mama called me back to the kitchen. "What'd he say?" she asked, though she normally stayed out of it.

"He wants me to come back."

She was pulling chicken off the bone, her hands covered in the sliminess. "Won't you cut some carrots and celery?" she asked. She had both bunches on the counter. I pulled out the cutting board from above the silverware drawer, standing shoulder to shoulder next to her.

"I'm not going back," I said with as much meaning as I could muster.

"Maybe he shouldn't call," she said, as if me telling him that would make him stop. The phone rang again. Mama was still working on the chicken, so I answered, my temples throbbing. It was Shane.

"Wanted to call and check in on how your mama's doing. I know the stuff with Danny is a lot for her."

"She's all right," I answered. I remembered that Dakota wanted me to get his birth date information and missed listening to what he was saying for a second.

"Charlie?"

"Oh, sorry, what was that?"

"I would like to stop by one afternoon this week, if that's all right?"

"Well, Mama's expecting you for supper one of these days," I replied, worried that she wouldn't get the chance to prepare him a proper meal.

"Of course. I just...well...I been meaning to come check on you, too."

And with that, Deputy Shane was going to be dropping in Friday afternoon. I wasn't going to be working that day. I just knew I was going to spend the week worrying about seeing him again. I went back to the kitchen where Mama was finishing the chopping I had started. She had talked to a lawyer earlier in the day and started telling me about it. She didn't understand why Danny's bail was so expensive since it was his first offense. Despite Mama's intentions and her declaration to God, we didn't have the money to get him out or to get him a decent lawyer. Danny had been moved to County, like Shane had said. And turns out there was so much evidence against him, they were encouraging him to take the first deal that would be offered.

"Mama, what he did is no small thing," I said as gently as I could, though all of our troubles were growing wearisome to me. Lenore's had been insane that day, and Jim's pleading had picked me raw like that chicken bone,

I woke up earlier than usual, but stayed in bed, my sheets warmed from my body and soft on my skin. It was still dark outside; my clock said 6:02 a.m. I turned on the lamp beside the bed and got out my notebook and pen so I could write down the dream I'd had, the corners of it still hanging to my barely awake mind.

This time I was in a hallway, like in high school, with lights flickering on and off. It was cold; the air was wet but I was sweating. There were many doors, and it was as if I was looking for a certain one. I remembered that I had something in my pocket that I needed. I reached in and pulled out a ring of keys. I held it up to the light to see all of them clearly.

Despite the wetness all around me, my throat was dry. The hall seemed to round out so I couldn't see the end. I found a water fountain and started to drink like I couldn't get enough. The water was sweet, and before I finished I woke up.

I wrote down all of the dream I could remember and wondered what in the world was going on with me. Shirley had said my subconscious was working out my problems, but why was I was sweating when it was so cold? What was the key for?

Shirley had also instructed me to try and fill up three full pages. She said she got the idea from a book called, "The Way of the Artist" or "The Artist's Way." I can't remember what the book was, but Shirley said she's been doing this "freewriting" for over a decade. "It's basically journaling, but the important thing is to fill up three notebook pages."

"Okay," I told her. I would try it.

"Changed my life," she said.

So I wrote and wrote full of thoughts of Shane and Jim. They were so different. And what was I going to do, go back to Jim? I thought if he died that would make it easier. I could grieve him and be done with it.

Then I thought about what was it that Shane wanted from me. He had him a girlfriend, as far as I knew. Even though Jim and Shane were nothing alike, I was the same. That much I knew.

After scribbling away, my hand cramped from all my writing, I stayed laying in bed for over an hour. The winter sun was rising outside my window, and I was grateful for the afghan my mama had made that kept the bed weighted and cozy. She had them all over the house, so no matter where you were, you could wrap yourself up and take a nap. I wanted her to teach me to make something like that. Yes, I needed to learn to make something, I decided, the thought turning into a necessity.

Just then Mama knocked on my door. "You up, Charlene? Coffee's ready."

"Be right there," I replied, getting out of bed suddenly lifted.

§

Later that week Mama let me take her car to pick up Shirley for the meeting. "Bet you didn't know I could drive," I joked, as she opened the door to get in.

"I still don't," she said, crossing herself, closing the car door. That made us giggle the whole way to the meeting. We had no way of knowing that it was going to be the night we would lose one, a sister of ours. Sitting in the wretched silence after Candy's husband barged into our meeting, screaming at her and all of us, was one of the darkest moments of my new life. Even the women who'd been around, freed from the bondage of the cycle of abuse for years, like Shirley and Willow and Jean, were leveled by the terror that man walked in the room with and the powerlessness with which Candy had followed him out.

Jean had called the police from the church office before the meeting ended. The two deputies who responded were older gray-hairs, bellies bulging over their belts.

"There's no record of a restraining order, ma'am," the slightly taller one said to Jean.

"He is her husband," he then said to his partner, as if agreeing that there wasn't anything they could do, or more correctly, would do.

"Well, y'all might as well just be about as useless as two pigs in slop," Jean spat.

"Agreed," Elizabeth Ann added, standing as tall as I'd seen her, glasses perched on her bird nose, looking ready to peck their badges off their uniforms. And then one after another, all of us ladies repeated the word, "Agreed," the cold air making our word visible like a rising smoke signal, a warning that rose above us and floated into the night sky.

The next day, Shane arrived at the house just after lunch. I was happy to see him, though I was still consumed with the events from the night before. I had busied myself that morning writing in my notebook the ick that had latched onto me like Velcro, as well as talking to Shirley on the phone for a good thirty minutes. I'd pretty much told her everything I'd written. Her ability to listen was like no other, and I felt comforted enough to move on to "the next indicated action," which is what she told me was all I had to do.

"Try and have a good time with Shane today. Be of service to your mama. She's going to be so thrilled having that young man, clean and with manners, in her house."

She went on to say that we'd have to have a powwow with Willow sometime to get deeper into the dreams and for me to keep writing them down. "All right," I replied. "Well, I better'd get ready."

"What is yours will come to you, hon," she said. He was coming all right.

"And put a prayer out there for Candy."

"Yes, of course."

I got off the phone, took a long bath, washing my hair, which was down to my shoulders. It had grown more in the last month than it had all the last year I was living with Jim. I'd always used the same VO5 shampoo, so it must have been the stress. It was like my hair knew more than I did.

Shane stood on the front porch with a bundle of red and pink flowers.

"These are for your mama," he said right as I was thinking they were for me. Then he unhid his other hand holding a smaller bunch. "And these are for you."

"Mama!" I called out into the house, not wanting him to see the roller coaster of hope my heart was riding.

We went on in the house, to the living room where the Christmas tree was lit by the front window. Mama met us, smiling as she saw the flowers he'd brought for her. "Are those Chrysanthemums? You shouldn't have, son. You sit down now, you hear? I'm going to put these in some water and be back out a minute with some snacks."

"Don't trouble yourself, Mrs. Montgomery," Shane started to say.

But she was already off down the hall with the flowers in her hands as if she'd won an award.

"That was real nice of you."

"My pleasure," he said eyeing me. I was suddenly struck by the thought that I had on too much makeup. And then too much perfume. I just knew I'd sprayed too much. It wasn't even mine. It was some of Mama's. Lily of the Valley. Oh, Lord. Did I smell like an old lady?

"So, how're you doing?" he asked. I motioned for him to have a seat. He sat on one end of the sofa, moving one of Mama's decorative, Santa pillows out of the way. I sat down next to him but not too close.

"I'm okay," which was true as I sat there looking at him. I saw how blue his eyes were, with a dark rim, intense, and they had me. "And you?" I managed.

He went on to tell me that he was quite busy with all that surprisingly showed up in our little town. He talked about how drugs were getting bad. Since we were in the mountains, people thought they could hide from the law. "Sure, it can make it harder once they get up in the woods, but hell,

I was born here. I've hunted these woods since I was a boy. I know 'em, right?"

I nodded, looking at the scruff on his face. I liked it. I was tempted to ask him about the woman he'd been with in Lenore's when Mama walked in carrying a tray. "Here, Mama, let me help," I said. She shrugged me off. She was in heaven. She could have carried the kitchen table out to us, she was so happy having him there. Shane stood up.

"I got it. Now, sit. Sit." She meant it.

Mama had a plate made of pimento cheese sandwiches with the crusts cut off. There were Christmas sugar cookies she'd made the night before and mugs of hot chocolate with baby marshmallows. Shane politely took a napkin and a triangle-shaped sandwich. I loved my mama's pimento cheese. I hadn't eaten before he came—I was too busy getting ready—so I found my mouth watering as soon as the creamy, tangy cheese hit my tongue.

Shane took a bite, too, and grinned at me. Mama hung around long enough to see that we were happy, not needing a thank you other than seeing Shane pick up a second triangle, and then left us alone to eat and chat.

Shane had another three sandwiches and a cookie in the shape of a tree, in a span of about five minutes. As he grabbed another cookie, "It's all right that I have another one?"

She'd be thrilled, I assured him. That woman loves a man to eat. After swallowing his last bite, he asked me about Jim.

"He calls," I said, reluctantly.

"Do you know what you're gonna do? As if it's any of my business, really."

"I don't," I said. "He's my husband, but… that's not right… I should know what to do."

"He hasn't…" he hesitated for a second then continued, "…threatened you at all, has he?" His concern caught me off guard. I was scared living with Jim, but I must have been in such a fog that the fear of him coming after me, well, I had pushed it away. I had maintained the thought he wouldn't have the guts to come to the house, so I'd be safe. And aside from him calling, he hadn't. Then thoughts of Candy's husband making a scene at our meeting flooded me, and I knew the fear was not as far from me as I pretended.

"He says he wants me to come back."

Shane and I took our cocoa and conversation to the porch to smoke.

"Let me grab my coat," I said and headed to the bedroom to grab it and check my face in the mirror.

It was a crisp cold outside, the colored lights from the tree through the window making colored patterns on the wooden railing.

"I don't mean to pry."

"And you?" I had to ask. "You seeing anybody?" He started to turn a little red. Willow had told me to be patient. I had messed that up twice now with him.

"Well, you know that woman you saw me with at Lenore's?"

"Yeah?" I was tingling and buzzing waiting for what he was going to say.

"We've been out a few times," he said. He shifted his weight, took a sip of his hot chocolate and looked past me like Danny had, staring at the tree-line.

My mind was on a spin cycle. Shane was just an old high school acquaintance; he was just being nice to a girl he'd known from back when. I had to get that into my head. I had to stop being so foolish thinking he wanted more with me.

It killed me that he wasn't saying. We stood there, not talking. He was so close. His bottom lip was fuller than the top, and I imagined it being nice to kiss. All I wanted from him was a gentle kiss, like I'd been craving for my whole life. Then I started worrying that I never would have one. It had only been a few months since I had been away from my terrible situation. I was still married! What the hell did I know about relationships?

He'd look at me and hold his gaze. There were moments I'd feel like something beyond us was having a conversation all to itself, like my dreams.

Then he had to go. He hugged me, more like my brother would have if he'd been a hugger. "Tell your mama if anything comes up with Danny's situation she doesn't understand, I'm happy to talk to her. And if Jim ever threatens you..." he said trailing off. "Thank your mama again for me, would ya?" My hope for more attention left with him, driving away in his police car.

"Y'all have a nice time?" Mama about whistled at me when I got back inside.

"He said thank you for the sandwiches."

She nudged me with her elbow as I brought the tray to the sink. "Well, he's certainly welcome. Anytime. Did you find out what Sunday he's available?"

"Oh, no, Mama. I can call him later."

"Next Sunday would be good. Ask him about then." Then she carried on singing. My mama had a pretty voice. She could carry a tune, unlike me. I thought she should sing in the choir at church but that was one of the positions she stayed away from. I suspect Daddy hadn't relished her singing like I did, and him being gone hadn't changed the weight of his opinion.

Years later, when I'd moved away, just thinking about her singing could make me cry. I wanted to hear her next to me in church, her mouth open in an O, her eyes looking toward the ceiling and to God.

§

It was in the early days of my meetings, in talks with Shirley and Willow, despite my distrust, I was encouraged to form some connection with God. The images I'd had were him as a man, like my mama believed. The subject seemed set in stone to her.

Mama had a picture or two of Jesus hung up in the house. One was in her room by the door and the other in the living room by a cherry side table, her favorite piece of furniture. She said it was over a hundred years old. It was the fanciest thing in the whole house, for sure, and young Jesus stood crowned in thorny roses above it.

I had been so mad at Mama's God and Jesus, but Shirley insisted that I needed to find a concept that would work for me. Really? I could do that? Just make up God? From what I could gather of her idea of God was in her sayings: "God is doing for you what you can't do for yourself," and "God don't make no junk." But she swore that came from somebody else.

Well, okay then. I was left to figure it out for myself. I used prayers like the Serenity Prayer because it was easy to memorize, and Shirley had told me to do it every night before bed on my knees (an act of humility). And then she said, "You just talk to him. Or her. Or whatever concept works. Must be loving and kind. And then you just talk and of course be sure and be quiet. Be sure to listen."

I never knew you could just have a conversation easy with God, like how I talked to Shirley.

19

I worked like a fiend at Lenore's, picking up every lunch shift I could, sometimes seven days a week. Shirley said it was good for me, that and being able to contribute to paying for food and stuff at Mama's. I'd never had to earn money before, so I was surprised to find that I was such a good worker. Lenore bragged to the others how well I kept the areas clean when I wasn't waiting on customers.

Dakota wasn't as dedicated to the working part of her job as I was. She and I made the most of our time by making up inside jokes about some of our regulars. For instance, the mayor came in all the time wearing a beanie with a propeller on top, like a 10 year old kid. He was the owner of the candy store on the other corner of Main and Broad. Then he'd go and tell some of the dirtiest jokes I'd think could be told.

Then we also had lawyers and judges coming in all the time, because we were right across from the courthouse. Those folks seemed stuck up to me. I recognized a few faces from high school such as Miller Woodside. He was a few years older than me, but I remember him because his daddy bought him a new red mustang, and it was one of the few new cars at our school. Most of us drove junk. I rode with Danny in his old truck until we both stopped going.

Miller couldn't have given two shits about who was serving his food. All he cared about was some big lawyer talk and making sure his sweet tea was full with a side glass of extra ice.

With Christmas being around the corner, me and Dakota found all the

Christmas sweaters we saw on the old ladies with their matching ornament earrings to be a right good joke. One lady had reindeer hanging from her lobes. We got to giggling fits so much that Lenore made us go to the back and get ahold of ourselves. She rarely scolded us, though. We got enough of that from Maryl and Ty. They couldn't be meaner during the rush. Ty screamed at me so bad one day, like Jim used to, all because I had let a customer's grilled ham 'n' cheese sit too long.

I wanted to punch him in the face for making me feel like a fuckup over a stupid sandwich. I was entering what Shirley called the "angry phase." She told me that I had lost my old way of living and had to grieve it, so I'd go through the Five Stages of Grieving. She said I was changing so fast my wheel bearings were going to come off.

§

One day Dakota came in to work, her cheek bruised. "What the hell happened to you?" I asked, though deep down I knew what.

"Nothing," she said quiet-like for the first time since I'd known her.

"What's Lenore gonna say? She ain't gonna let you work like that."

"I fell, okay?" she said, her freckles ruddy with a flush of shame.

"I'm sorry. I didn't mean to." I didn't want to make her feel worse and knew Lenore wouldn't believe her lie. It amazed me that since the beginning of time, when man started taking his frustrations and hardships out on woman that we'd have, by now, come up with some new explanations and excuses. But no. We use the same old sorry stories.

I knew Lenore wouldn't let Dakota work her shift. Soon as she walked in, took one look at the purple and blue on Dakota's face, her mouth became stiff and straight-lined. She took Dakota gently by the arm into her little office in back. When Dakota came out, she had been crying. Lenore patted her on the back and said, "I'm gonna call to see if you made it, so you best not, not go."

Dakota nodded, avoiding eye contact with me, got her purse and headed out. Lenore, seeing my face said, "She'll be okay. Don't worry. I'm gonna make sure of it." I knew she'd do what she said, but the whole of it made me sick to my stomach. I headed outside to smoke and calm myself.

"Hey, hon!" a familiar voice called to me from across the street.

"Why, hey!" I managed to call back with effort, though relieved as hell to see Shirley and Willow making their way over to my side of the street. Willow got to me first and gave me one of her hugs. With that, I couldn't help myself. The tears I'd been holding in came pouring over. Through the tears, I told them about Dakota's face.

"It's okay, hon," Shirley said a couple of times. "Lenore's probably sent her to the Safe Depot to talk to somebody."

They told me that work was the best thing I could be doing and to go and be productive. They said they'd be back at 12:30 to celebrate Willow finishing the painting of her foyer—a hallway, as Shirley explained to me. They seemed certain that Lenore would take care of Dakota.

When Shirley and Willow showed back up to have lunch, Lenore stayed at their table for a good fifteen minutes. I hadn't known they knew each other that well. But I was starting to put together Shirley telling me to use her name on my application and me getting the job. Them knowing each other gave me the courage after work to ask Lenore about the Safe Depot.

I finished cleaning up the salad station, covering the leftover dressing in Saran Wrap and putting away the extra bucket of lettuce. I took my tickets and cash to the bar where she was sitting counting them up for the day.

She began by telling me that she'd called the house and Dakota had indeed stopped by. "That's good," I said still not understanding where Dakota was sent to. "So what happens there?"

"It's a safe place women can go to when they got to get out and got no other place to go," she explained. "There's people to talk to who've been through similar situations," she continued, not looking up from the spreadsheet she was adding numbers to.

"And you run that and the restaurant here, too?"

"Yes, I do. I started it when my daughter's husband killed her."

"I'm so sorry." I already knew her story from Shirley, but to hear it from Lenore was different.

"Yeah, well, I wouldn't wish it on anyone. And here we are. Willow's volunteered for me a time or two," she added. "I assume you know her story?"

"Yeah. I do," I replied, imagining Dakota driving up and Willow greeting her there the way she greeted new women at our meetings. Under normal circumstances, I'd have said she and Dakota would hit it off. But not that day. Having seen Dakota's face, with a huge black eye and swollen lip, I wasn't so sure a big grin was what she would be up for.

"We can also provide them with numbers for free legal advice, or child care," Lenore went on. She said they got grants and donations to cover their costs.

I stammered a bit before telling her that I'd just gotten out of a bad situation myself. She didn't seem surprised. I thought how she had to have a kind heart to run the Safe Depot but wasn't the kind of person to show it. She came across tough.

"Well, Charlie, you need anything you can always go by there, you know? Stop by anytime." On a scratch piece of paper she wrote down the address. "Don't be passing this around. We got to keep it quiet, the location and all."

"All right," I said and thanked her. It was time for me to head out. I walked to my car in back of the old brick building that was the restaurant. As I rounded the corner, I almost blacked out from seeing Jim in his truck parked next to my car. Fuck. He was smoking a cigarette, had grown a beard, and looked awfully skinny to me. I knew it wasn't from missing my cooking, that's for sure. All the phone calls I was getting hadn't done squat to prepare me to see him.

"Charlie, baby," he said coolly. I didn't want to look at him but couldn't look away. "Wow. I sure missed seein' you."

All the blood in my body rushed to my head. My hands started to shake, and I was overcome by rage. It was as if the desperation I'd felt in my kitchen the last time I'd seen him, when I was begging for him to eat the goddamn biscuits I had made, had disappeared into an underground well, deep inside me, a growing monster in wait. Knowing where jealousy and crazy had taken me before, ready to kill him, I was relieved when my body made its way to my car. Jim had gotten out of his truck and was making his way over to me when he saw I wasn't going to respond to his hollering. I slammed the door so fast I about caught his hand in it.

"Goddammit, Charlie. You're my fucking wife!" His voice was wild and for a second the beast of my anger went still. I almost turned the engine off, climbed out, and went to him. To my surprise, the words of the Serenity Prayer cranked up in my head, like the winding of a music box. I said the words out loud, over and over and over and over again, my knuckles turned white from gripping the steering wheel.

As I sped off, I hoped to God he wouldn't follow me. I looked back in my rear-view mirror, seeing him standing in the middle of the street yelling at me like he used to. The difference was I was the one leaving.

Without a thought, I drove straight to the police station, just across Broad Street and two blocks up Oakwood. I pulled in between two police cars and sat in my car, a terrified me working to get ahold of my breath. And then I saw Jim's truck slow down just outside the parking lot before peeling off. I sat there blank-faced and pale.

A minute later, Shane came out of the station talking to another officer. He spotted me, said something to the guy he was with, then came over to my car. He was clean-shaven and had on his uniform. God, he was handsome. I was sure I looked like pure shit. I would have cared more if I wasn't scared numb.

I opened the door to the car. The air hit me, wet and cold. "Charlie, what's wrong?" he said standing in front of me.

"Jim," I said and then burst into tears. He put his arms around me and held me as I sobbed. He continued to hold me. Then I was aware that his name badge was pricking my chest. I realized how hard I'd been hanging onto him. I needed a tissue. Shane pulled out his hanky and handed it to me.

I looked up at him and his eyes were like deep holes, like the wild woman cave I had entered when I was having that vision in the hospital. I wanted to fall in. They belonged to a man, a safe man. It wasn't but a second later that my thoughts flipped. It occurred to me once again that he was just being nice. He was comforting a broken woman because he was a good man. I'd done met a good one and started to think it meant something special.

What a mess I was. What a huge fucking mess. "Thank you," I managed and started to hand him back his hanky then thought better of it. "Can I wash this and give it back later?"

"That's fine. You gonna be okay?" he asked. I lied the obvious lie that I would. "You need protection, Charlie," he told me, but I was too drained, once again, to want to think about it, to make a decision.

"I don't think he'll do anything," I said, knowing that with recent events like with Candy, Dakota getting smacked around, and Jim showing up outside my work, I wasn't so sure what wasn't going to happen. I tried to change the subject by telling him how my mama had enjoyed him coming to her house and wanted me to invite him over for Sunday supper coming up, but he wouldn't let it go. "Why don't you get a restraining order? You could do that now."

"Naw....Can't." I couldn't.

"You don't need him showing up like that anymore," as if that was that. He was right but I told him I'd have to think about it.

"Yes, I can come over Sunday. Make sure to wash that good, will ya'?" I managed to smile. For the time being, I was scheduled to meet Shirley at her house and was already late.

§

George was at work, so Shirley and I had the house to ourselves. It was a log cabin built "way long ago," she'd told me, and they had done a lot of renovations on it before moving in. It was nothing like Willow's house. All her colors were spring, where Shirley was an autumn. There was a fireplace in the kitchen that went through the wall to the living room. Shirley had what looked like mini-spider webs, hanging on the windows of the living room. She told me they were dreamcatchers. There was a massive watercolor of a wolf howling at the moon over the mantel. Not much was decorated for Christmas.

Shirley said Shane was right, after I told her why I was late. "A restraining order is a fine idea," she said.

She asked me if I'd thought about what I wanted to do about my marriage situation. "No, I haven't really," I admitted, feeling ashamed.

She told me it was completely understandable, and that it was still rather fresh for me. I was probably in a kind of shock still, she explained. She went on to tell me that it could be a good state to be in, to take care of all the business that went into leaving one's husband.

"Let's start with getting him to give you some room. You can talk to the women at Lenore's place for more information, but in the meantime..." Shirley said she'd go to the police station with me the next day, and we'd take the first step of filling out the paperwork together. She said too that it was empowering for me to make those types of decisions and to follow through with action doing what I could. "You know," she said as she patted my arm, "the courage to change the things we can."

Mama was up for all kinds of reasons by the time I got home, mostly worrying about Christmas being around the corner, the church in a frenzy, and Danny's law trouble, her having to meet with the appointed defense attorney. I told her that we would have company on Sunday after all. She was hanging up the extra lights she had driven all over town for, getting the special colored kind she was most fond of. The house had to look just so.

Mama would say that Christmas wasn't about cut pine trees, glass balls, and strung-up popcorn and berries but about the birth of her beloved Jesus Christ. Though by the time Christmas was well on its way, the house would be dressed up like a firework burst frozen in the sky.

§

In the spirit of her Jesus, that Friday she had me take her by the church and pull the tag of a kid from the Giving Tree that we'd buy clothes and toys for.

The tag I picked had the handwritten name Rose. She was nine. She wanted a Barbie, some outfits, a new jacket size small, and a hat and matching mittens. Mama said we'd get her some barrettes and other hair goodies, too. We agreed that I'd go down to Kmart Saturday after work to get what was on her list.

I thought about little Rose's situation. I'm sure somebody at the church knew her and her family, if she had one. Everything would be wrapped the same and labeled "From Santa" so she wouldn't know the presents were from us and not from her parents or jolly ol' Saint Nick. The whole thing made me think back to my early Christmases and how much worse it could have been. Daddy would sit in a chair in the living room as Mama pulled presents from under the tree. For some reason, it was the one day Daddy pretty much kept his mouth shut. We never got a lot of presents, but in thinking of Rose, I counted my blessings. I always had a warm coat.

On the phone, I mentioned my thoughts about Rose to Shirley. She said she'd go shopping with me. I got worried that Mama would feel slighted by me going without her, given it was her idea, but she was busy when I told her, so she showed no bother.

"Fine. Fine," she said as she turned back to sifting through her recipes for pork chops, which is what we'd be serving Shane.

§

On our way to Kmart that weekend, I told Shirley I wanted to check on Dakota. She hadn't been back to the restaurant since Wednesday. I supposed Lenore wanted her face to heal before waiting on customers. I wanted to call her but had never gotten her number. I didn't think it was right to ask Lenore for it, so I didn't. I asked Shirley what she thought I should do. "You could invite her to Thursday night," she suggested. I hadn't even thought of that and wasn't sure how I felt about it. If Dakota didn't like the meeting, well, I didn't want her to spoil it for me.

"Maybe it was a one-time thing for her."

"We know 'bout that, don't we, hon?" Shirley replied.

§

That night before bed, a rise of panic began making its way up the back of my throat, whispering in my ear as if it were a light draft moving in through a window. Thank God Shirley had warned me. "Sabotage can show up when you're headed in the right direction. Watch for it."

I thought, "How could that be?" I was doing my best to do right, and Shirley agreed saying I was taking huge steps, one of them being not going back to Jim. "It seems logical, what with him acting out. But we both know this isn't about logic. So don't discount that, Charlie. That there's a smack in your face miracle," she'd said.

So just as I was in the bathroom washing my face, that underground voice full of pain started in on me. I looked in the mirror and stared a minute too long. I had broken out across my forehead. My hair was a ratty mess. I am a slug, I thought. Who would ever want that? I knew I must be insane to think Shane had any interest.

I was disgusted by my reflection in the mirror. I hadn't been touched by a man, other than a slamming fist across my face, a fuck with a stranger in the woods, or a sympathy hug in over a year and a half. I held onto the porcelain sink losing balance. I knew I was less-than.

I managed to crawl into bed, wondering how in the hell I was going to get some relief. I was bored of saying prayers and writing. "What is the point of waking up again?" I wondered. All my sorrows must have tired me, and I drifted off.

Next morning, as I lay in bed awake, scared to go back to the bathroom and see my face in the mirror again, I remembered my dreams. I'd had two. One about Jim and the other Shane.

From the first, all I remember was Jim standing there tall and strong beside me. He said, "Follow me." He sounded convincing, clear and calm. He pulled me to him and that was that.

The second was me going into Shane's house. I'd never been in his house in real life, but in my dream I was going back in, familiar, with a key he'd given me. I opened the door to his bedroom and was surprised to see him asleep in his bed. More of a shock was a small, blonde girl cradled in his arm beside him.

Oh, God. I turned to leave quick. Before I got turned all the way around, I saw him open an eye. My heart almost stopped. I was humiliated thinking he saw me creeping on him. I was relieved that it had only been a dream.

Laying there in the coccoon of the warm blankets, the dull light of the morning sun peering through the curtains' lace, I came to realize the dreams were messages for me. Shirley had said as much, but it's that thing of needing to experience something for oneself until it clicks. I could see that the first was Jim trying to get me to come back to him. The second dream was telling me to let Shane go, the idea of him and me, if nothing else. He'd been so sweet to me but wasn't doing anything to date me. He'd never asked me out. Still, I didn't feel quite ready.

If I canceled Sunday supper after all the work Mama had done, she'd be crushed. Then there was the trouble with Danny and the law. We needed him to help us. I couldn't do that to Mama, either. And then with Jim coming after me, well, I needed to have him around to protect me. There were too many reasons to not do anything. Maybe the timing wasn't right, I decided.

My back and forth thinking—"mental masturbation," Jean had said one night outside a meeting—was driving me to Nutsville. I heard Mama in the kitchen. She was getting ready for church. I couldn't be bothered going with her. But I got up and went to the kitchen for coffee.

"You're not ready, Charlene."

"I ain't going this morning, Mama," I said pouring myself a cup.

"You go to them meetings at that Lutheran church ever week, Charlene. The least you could do is attend Sunday service at Mount Tabor, where you were baptized."

"That's different, Mama. I don't feel like arguing with you. I've been to church regular now for weeks. One week ain't gonna hurt." She pursed her lips, unconvinced. "I'll finish getting the house ready," I said, hoping that would work.

"Everything that needs to be done has been done," she replied with her drawn-on eyebrows crinkled up, fed up with me.

"Fine," I huffed. "I'll get ready."

"Don't you get sassy with me, now, ya' hear?" She walked out of the kitchen. This was our first fight in some time, and it felt awful. Things had been sweet between us. Sabotage. Shirley's warning. I took my mug of coffee with me to the bathroom to work on my face, covering the splotches best I could and brushing the uselessness of my hair. It was untamable, like the loathsome feeling I couldn't out-think.

§

Church turned out to be not as bad as I had feared, so much that it was some relief being there singing Christmas carols and listening to Pastor Eppleby bring us just a little bit closer to the birth of Christ. After the service, the kids got excited as people told fibs about Santa coming. I overheard one small boy tell elder Mr. Jenkins about a new cow he'd be getting.

The boy showed he was nearly "this many" as he held up one hand plus the thumb on his other hand to Mr. Jenkins who put on a show of being impressed with the idea of getting a cow for Christmas at the age of six. "You gonna ride it?" he teased.

"No!" the little boy shouted back. "You don't ride cows! You feed them and then milk them!"

What the boy didn't know was that his granddaddy, a descendent of Albert L. Pemberton of South Carolina, got his grandkids, five before that one, a cow all right. But that cow wasn't no milking cow. And it wasn't going to be living too long after ol' Santa dropped it off Christmas morning.

On the ride home from church, I thought about Danny and the last Sunday I'd seen him when he first got locked up in the local jail. Mama had visited him in County without me. She'd talked to his lawyers and was told it didn't look good for him but, yes, they'd do all they could to get him the minimum sentence. All-in-all, the process could take a year.

We got home with enough time to set the table and put the creamed corn, sweet yam casserole, and rolls in the oven to warm. Mama had been right in that there wasn't much left to do. Her iron skillet was sitting proudly, stove top, ready to fry up the porkchops she'd pulled out of the fridge. Laid out on the counter was Crisco and a bowl of mashed and seasoned bread crumbs.

Mama had a hand-written list of what else needed to go on the table. She tended to cook double for the people she was serving. So, she had the list to make sure no side of sweet pickles or beet salad got left tucked away in the refrigerator. "A man needs to eat and to eat good," she'd say. I had failed my mama in more ways than I could keep track but me not cooking was the main one.

I tried to pretend I wasn't getting excited to see Shane, especially since I'd loosely considered forgetting about him. But life began to feel more bearable, my earlier condition slipping out the back, off somewhere beyond the tree line, the closer the clock got to the half hour. By 1:20, I was buzzing. I think Mama noticed, but my guess is she accounted it to me having attended church that morning. Which, I'm sure, she gave Jesus and herself a bit of credit for.

§

After the last bite of pecan pie, Shane told us a story about when he was a new lawman. Said he was running after a half-naked man in the woods, hound dogs yelping signals in the dark. He was with another officer, fairly new also, and they had accidentally stumbled upon the criminal activity of a man running a still, moonshine. That was only half of the story.

Before that, he told us they'd gotten a call that another man had crossed the state line with something really illegal. Shane wouldn't say exactly what, maybe too close to our own situation with Danny, but the way he described it, me and Mama were entertained. He said he and his buddy had set out to prove themselves by chasing after the really bad guy through the woods and, as it had been a moonless night, how they couldn't see jack.

The dogs had led them to the still and then on a chase farther into the woods. He said that tackling a half-naked man wasn't what he'd envisioned upholding the law to be. He said they had been determined, though. "I did what I had to do." His eyes crinkled at the edges as he smiled. "Yeah, we never did catch that other guy."

That gave me and Mama a good laugh. That woman had her hanky out, the one with Daddy's initials, wiping back tears. We must have needed it.

I had the urge to reach my hand out and touch Shane's arm. Instead, I sat tight. The way he looked at me, though, was as if the whole lightness of his shoulders and face were because of me. "Yep. That's Charlene right there," Mama said when he looked behind me at a tiny photograph on the wall. It was of me and Danny, who was behind me in the picture, pushing me on my red tricycle.

"I bet that thing's still in the shed, rusty as all get out," I said, not remembering the day of the picture but knowing what it took for Mama to let go of something. She still had Daddy's clothes hanging in the closet.

"Ya'll can take a look for it after supper, if you'd like," Mama said. "She loved it, Shane. Sure did. Had to pull her off of it every time. She'd holler, would she ever." I was sad to not remember that day. I thought, Wow, it all started with a tricycle—my attachment to men was the same. Then Mama looked at me as if I might owe her an apology for being so hard-headed even as a child.

"Well, Mama," I said wanting to change the subject. Lord knows I owed that woman lots of apologies for lots of hard-headedness, but Shirley said they wouldn't mean anything until I really changed on the inside and that would take time.

"Yes, well then," she replied all giddy. Shane was polite enough to not bring up Danny. We didn't mention him even as he was staring back at us from the picture, wearing his pulled-up striped socks and dorky grass green short shorts. I was too young to look that goofy, unlike the album from a later time that I prayed to God stayed tucked away in a side drawer.

A couple of times as we talked there in the kitchen, I thought I caught Shane looking at me, like he was taking me in. Then I'd doubt it, thinking I was making it up. Then I thought, "Well, how could he be in Mama's kitchen?" And then I had to keep reminding myself he was there for her. I told myself he just felt sad that she was an old woman who'd reared two sorry children.

He tried to help her carry the dishes over to the sink. She shooed him off and told him not to be silly. No guest in my mama's house was going be clearing the table. Again, especially no man. "Your mama's a sweet lady, Charlie," he said as we headed down the hall toward the porch.

"Can be," I replied pretending to punch him in the arm. There I went again, playing the tomboy. My mama had wanted a girlie girl, and aside from liking china dishware, I turned out to be anything but, and it sure wasn't getting me what I wanted.

21

Christmas had came and gone. I had helped Mama take down the decorations, unraveling what seemed like miles of lights off of the tree and front porch and then raveling them back in loops to be stored away in the shed. We wrapped her Santa and poinsettia pillows in plastic bags and stuffed them "neatly" in Danny's old bedroom closet. It took us nearly an entire afternoon.

Mama went about acting like Danny was in a hospital for some fatal illness the way she prayed and insisted everyone she knew pray for him as well. His name went on the list every week at Mount Tabor. I thought, "Mama, they know your boy's in jail for armed robbery."

Under regular circumstances, she wouldn't want anybody to know, especially not them gossipy hens in her circle, but she was convinced that the Devil had gotten a hold of her son, and it was our Christian duty, a test of her faith, to pray for her son's safe return to Christ's loving arms.

Danny was headed to prison, even if the courts took their sweet time sentencing him. He would be sitting in County for up to a year, but with his case, could be there by spring. Instead of praying for my brother, I'd written him a couple of special letters I never sent. I was angry at him.

I'd written Shane about a hundred love letters, never mailed nor left on his windshield. They were my version of love letters, anyway. One of them, I poured my heart into until I had tears rolling down my cheeks. I'm sure I looked all dramatic like one of them actresses in the old movies I watched when I lived in the trailer.

My night dreams and Shirley both told me over and over to let go of Shane. I wanted to do right, let go, but there was a piece in the back of my mind that kept hanging on. I told Shirley that in a way it was a form of hope and that couldn't be too bad, right? She called that kind of thinking "rationalizing." I put as much fantasy into him as I had before Jim and I were married. Shirley called it "obsession." She had big words for every way I thought.

Mama didn't help it none. She and I never talked about the future, like when I was going to move out. I could feel that her hope was that Shane was the man who was going to rescue me.

"Oh, Mama," I wish I could have said to her, "I want that, too. But he's hot, then cold, then absent." I mean, that Sunday he'd come to dinner, before Christmas, I thought for sure he'd try to kiss me as he was leaving. Instead, it was like somebody walked in his head and turned some light switch off and he never did, and I hadn't seen him since. I was learning that I couldn't let go of something until it became more painful to hang on. It was getting more painful.

§

I picked up Shirley to drive us to the meeting that week. She got in the car with a tissue in her hand and her eyes were puffy. "What is it?" I asked.

"That woman, Candy. Maybe you should pull over a minute."

"Oh no." I knew what Shirley was going to tell me. I got chills along my arms.

"Candy's husband killed her. Shot her while she was sleeping."

"Jesus," I mumbled as I pulled over right at Maple Street past the same hundred-year old red oaks that had witnessed me and the pistol in the seat where Shirley sat.

"And then he turned it on himself. Just the most horrible thing. The most horrible..." Shirley kept saying.

I was stunned. I was getting how we could die from this—our warped minds constantly working one over on us. Lord, I hoped Jim wasn't that desperate. Shirley must have sensed what I was thinking because she responded to my quietness by putting her hand on my shoulder.

I gathered myself and cranked the car. We drove past the library and along the road that ran behind the buildings of the hardware store, a jewelry store and the coffee shop and into the parking lot of the church. "Now, don't you go worrying about nothing, dear. That's why you got that restraining order." It was the first time I didn't believe her.

A small group of the women were standing outside hugging and crying. Willow grabbed me and squeezed me with all her might, all of her hopeful grins and smiles lost. She had been the closest to Candy. Instead of crying, I smoked, except I was trembling so badly, I couldn't steady my hand to get the damn cigarette to my lips.

"Let's go inside," Elizabeth Ann suggested gently. It couldn't have been more than forty degrees and it was well past 5:30, the usual start time. What we ended up having that night was more of a vigil for Candy, a woman I had met only a handful of times but had a bellyful of sorrow for as if she'd been my sister.

_____22_____

Dear Jim,

You fucking asshole. Bastard. What did you go and do that for? Why'd you have to pick me at that party? Why the fuck didn't you just leave me alone that night? I could have had a better life never knowing you. Fuck you. I'm not sorry. Fuck. You sorry bastard.

That was one of the many letters I wrote Jim after the fucker had drowned himself. Nobody to send them to. Damn him. Shirley had told me to write them anyway. I didn't anticipate that my husband, after five months of being separated, would get so drunk and high, row himself out to the middle of Chicory Holler Lake under a full bright moon and tumble himself into it. They say it was an accident. That meant, of course, that I had a funeral to attend in the following week, because I was still legally his wife. Now I had to deal with the Wilsons. None of it was something I wanted to face.

I had gotten pretty good at putting my tattered thinking on paper by the time Jim had stupidly died. But I couldn't out-write my feelings any more than I could out-think them running around in my head. They had to be walked through no matter what. I couldn't get away from how bad it hurt, even when I'd at one point thought him dying would be my salvation.

Up until then, between the Sunday dinner before Christmas with Shane and Mama, Candy getting killed and the morning a patrol car pulled into the yard, not Shane, to deliver the news of Jim's drowning, I'd been living my life best I could. I was working at Lenore's cafe and going to my Thursday women's meetings. It was a simple life, but I had become too high strung for much else. The cafe wore me out. There was enough drama during the day. My once-a-week meeting brought me my comfort. Us women in the group were now bonded more than ever.

§

Mama wasn't asking for much money from me to stay in her house, but she did expect me to get closer to Jesus. One way was to attend church regular. The other was to give a good chunk of what I earned to the church. "It's called tithing, Charlene Louise. You give to God because he's been so generous with us."

Ha! I managed to not laugh in her face. I thought that was the biggest crock of shit, myself, but I only shared those feelings with Shirley. Boy, did I get a surprise. "Your mama's got a point."

"You foolin' me?" I thought for sure she was messing with me. One look at her face, though, and it was clear she was as serious as the day was long.

"Spiritual is always first."

"But what does God care about money?"

"It's a gesture. An offering. Don't have to be to the church," she spoke gently. It meant, too, that Shirley tithed since she only spoke from her experience. She could tell I was still hung up. "What?" she asked.

"Well..." I hesitated. "But because God's so generous?"

"Oh, you mean because of all the hurt and suffering in the world?"

She got it. "Yes!"

"Good question. That's common to wonder. Suffering seems to be part of the human condition, huh?"

"I just get so pissed at God for all the bullshit. You know I've tried praying since leaving Jim. But for what Mama went through? For my sorry-ass Daddy? For my brother being all fucked up to go to jail, for Lenore's daughter to be murdered by her husband, for Willow's mama torturing her daddy? For Candy who was murdered by her husband when she was trying to get away from the son of a bitch? For Jim being such an asshole and..."

Before I knew it, snot was pouring from my nose, tears pouring from my eyes. I didn't care. I kept on. "The man I was crazy about beat the shit outta me! He NEVER wanted me. He didn't love me! Then the other man that God puts into my life, he don't give a fuck neither. He don't want me, nobody wants me. And I'm supposed to pay God because he's so fucking generous? Well...FUCK GOD!"

At that, I startled myself straight. The tears stopped. It was like a heavy late summer storm, fast and loud, crackly and scary, and then gone less than ten minutes. I wiped the water from my eyes and that damn woman was smiling so big I thought I must need to wipe my nose or something.

"What?" I demanded.

"Girl. Good for you." Was she as insane as I was? Did she not hear me? "God can take it," she said and continued to smile at me, nodding and patting my hand.

I went back and forth on the prayer thing, whether it worked and in what ways. But what came as a surprise to me was that after my "Fuck God Moment," some of my praying seemed to be delivering. I don't mean that it gave me everything I thought my life was missing: a man, a house, my own family, a car, and money. My list could go on. But like the comfort I was getting from the meetings, the women in my circle when we huddled close together, and at night when I turned to sleep, well, those things were delivering me from self-hate just enough to keep me showing up in my own life, whatever the circumstances. And I had been praying for relief, and I was continuously being surrounded by strength and love. I couldn't keep denying that. Also, it got me through attending Jim's funeral.

§

Shirley drove me to the gravesite and squeezed my hand before we walked through the grass to where Jim's coffin sat perched, still above ground. I could see my breath in the February cold. The first person I saw was Jim's mama. They had her a chair, like a throne, set up by the dirt hole and her hefty self was sitting high and mighty in it. Jim's daddy was standing, shoulders square beside her. Then there was a tall man dressed in a black dress coat, black pants and tie next to Jimmy Senior holding a piece of paper. He must have been with the funeral home. There were a number of other folks there, most I didn't recognize. A couple of his old buddies. Nobody looked at me. It's like I didn't exist and wasn't still his wife.

The ground was soft from rain earlier in the week and was like a suction cup to my dress shoes. I did not want to get stuck there. "I would leave my shoes right there in the mud if I had to," I thought.

There was no way my mama would have come, as nobody was going to mention Jesus, and she was sure Jim was headed to hell. She wanted no part in that. However, Mama had made sure I went out and got an appropriate black dress for the occasion and told me to "be sure and wear some light lipstick so you look nice."

"It's not a date, Mama."

"Don't sass me, Charlene Louise." And yet when I was standing on the front porch, smoking, waiting for Shirley's longbed to come up the drive, my mama came out beside me and handed me her hanky, the one with Daddy's initials, and a little black purse to put it in.

"Thank you, Mama," I said. She knew I meant more than those two words could say.

§

In the days following Jim's death, going forward with my life as a widowed, ex-battered wife, Shirley suggested that in addition to prayer, that I find some recreation and hobbies. I was stumped as to what that would be for me. It was no surprise that she had me get out my notebook and start writing. "Make a list without thinking too much," she said. "Start with ten ideas of what you like to do."

I thought she'd flipped, telling me to come up with that many ideas, "quick-like, without thinking," but I did what she suggested, because so far she'd been right about, well, everything. "I'm just passing down what was suggested to me," she said. She never took credit.

Number one on my list was makeup and doing hair. Then watching old movies came to mind, so that was number two. I thought maybe I could write a movie, since I was so good at living in fantasy. That was number three on my list. Didn't know diddly about how, but Shirley had said, "Quick-like." I thought I might keep idea number three to myself—me writing a movie seemed like pure fantasy in itself. But I ended up reading the list to Shirley, all of it, and when I did get to movie writing, she just smiled and nodded as if it was a tremendous idea.

Number ten on the list was making crafts. "I like that one, the crafts," she said. "What kind?"

"Like, I don't know. Painting something on wood, like a sign or something?"

"That sounds right to me. Start there. Becoming a screenwriter might come later then."

I asked Mama if it was okay for me to spend some of my money, the leftover after tithing, which I'd started, on my new crafts projects. I still wasn't paying much towards living in her house, so felt getting her blessing was the right thing to do. "You don't need to ask me," she assured me.

We had an art store in town called Patton's Art Supply that belonged to Mrs. Gillian Patton, who had been my art teacher in elementary school. She never had any kids, but I remembered liking her a lot. And I remembered how she had especially taken to some of my drawings from her sixth-grade class.

When I walked in, I saw that her store was full of real art supplies for real artists. She came over to me and we introduced ourselves.

"I remember you," she said. "Charlie, is it?" I felt a brief wash of shame, as if maybe she didn't think I was so great at drawing after all and somehow I'd remembered it all wrong.

"Yes, ma'am."

"Oh, you can call me Gillian." With that she whirled me up and down the aisles pointing out charcoals and special pencils with different lead types, explaining their uses to me. She showed me pastels, which were expensive as crap for something that was like a chalky crayon, but she told me that Rembrandt were the good ones. "Smooth," she said. I told her I didn't have much money to spend and that I was looking to get into crafts.

"Well, you'd need to go to the craft store for that, dear. This here's a Fine Arts store." Any hope I'd had that I was on the right track slipped, like jam sliding down my face.

"Aw, now, don't look so forlorn. It's all right," she said. "You should play with charcoal instead. You could draw, I remember."

That made me feel a little better. But I still had to ask, "How much?" I couldn't help thinking I was in the wrong place. I thought for sure it wasn't going be affordable to someone like me.

"We'll get you a few pieces to start and a less pricey pad. You'll need an eraser, too." She pulled out supplies for me and showed me the price, as if she'd decided that I could afford it, that I would afford it.

"Never used charcoal."

"Just play with it, Charlie. Can you do that?" I nodded. I didn't know if I could "play" with it, but I was willing to try. She rang me up. As she did, she explained how the eraser wasn't the same as a Number 2 pencil eraser. "You dab it on the paper." Then she said, "You know I have people over on Tuesday nights to visit and draw. You should come." I was beginning to feel like it was too much, my new adventure into the world of art. In that moment, I wished I had known that there was a difference in stores of those for crafts and those that weren't.

"I don't know."

"You can decide later. Been having it for a while now. Will still be having it when you're ready."

As I was gathering up my new supplies, she gave a few more instructions to get me started. She told me to pay attention to the lines of an object rather than the object itself. Sounded to me like Shirley talking. I didn't understand exactly what she meant, like how to look at a line without thinking, "That there's a roll of toilet paper," which is one of the objects she suggested I start with. Didn't seem like art to me. Maybe New York City art or something. Mama was going to think I had lost my senses spending time staring at a roll of toilet tissue. But I thanked Mrs. Gillian for her help. She was such a kind lady, she was.

I was going to run the "art class" idea by Shirley, who had more than once told me that she wasn't there to give me permission for what to do. I could do what I wanted whenever. Truth was, I was too scared to make a decision by myself. I felt I needed her help in just about everything from taking an art class in my old teacher's house to how much money to donate to whether or not driving by the police station before and after work to catch a glimpse of Shane was a good idea or not. I couldn't seem to come to some of the most obvious conclusions by myself. She said that would change with time.

23

I was overjoyed when Dakota came back to the restaurant from the Safe Depot and was working with me again. She seemed different somehow, though, as if her heart had been punctured. She was more serious and would talk about her Saturn return or something, saying that it was a big old planet that made everything heavy, deep, and long lasting. "It's a lesson I gotta learn and not all lessons are fun or pretty," she'd say.

I didn't have it in me to tell her a little bit of lightness, some laughter, couldn't hurt. Seeing her cope on her own made me know, deep down, how lucky I was to have my group. I wished Dakota would come but she would insist she had too much of an independent spirit to become dependent on some group.

I tried not to take it personally. I knew I could not have survived without Shirley, Willow, Elizabeth Ann, and the others. Even the women when they would come in in full crisis and wouldn't stay seemed to help me. I could not explain it to Dakota.

Sandy stayed coked up 24/7, which you would think would make her jumpy and unpredictable. Just the opposite. She was the best waitress, even with all her bathroom breaks, and finally warmed up to me after a full two months of barely a word to split between Dakota and me. For some reason on one of our smoke breaks before a lunch shift, I told Sandy about my brother, his using and armed robbery. She had asked where I was from, if I had any family and such. I skipped telling her about Jim but, "Yes, I got a Mama and brother still around. Well, sort of." We were doing that dance where you don't look at each other too much out on the sidewalk by the back of the cafe. But I saw that had got her attention. So, I told her about Danny's situation. That is when she told me her husband had done seven years for selling drugs back in the eighties.

"We were newly married and same as Danny. He'd gotten himself arrested," Sandy said. "But I loved him no different because he was my soulmate and I'd have waited twenty years for him." Then she threw her cigarette on the ground, put it out with her black work loafer and headed back inside.

I wasn't figuring how she was still getting high all the time, with the risk that could be for him to go back. But I was able to figure it was none of my business. I was thankful she had a similar experience as me and told me so.

Along with Sandy being way up and Dakota being way down, I was having a harder time with the cooks, Maryl and Ty. Lord, what bag of nails you got stored up your hineys, I wondered every dang day. The two of them had attitude to spare. I did not know how Lenore, who ran a shelter for battered women, for God's sake, could hire two sons of bitches to run her kitchen.

"Fucking useless," Maryl cussed at me one day, nearly loud enough for people coming in the front door to hear, all for not getting the food out "right this second!" I had just been triple sat and was already covering for poor Ida who was busy with her ten-top getting drink orders. I only had two hands and two feet, for Christ's sake. I wanted to take her out in the middle of the kitchen.

Ty, well, he was just a boy really, but I could see his meanness brewing early. His dumb girlfriend, though very pretty, hung out at the bar every day waiting for him to pay her some mind. He'd ignore her until it was time to go. I saw too much of me in her and knew it was his meanness that made her hang around like a lost puppy. I did a lot of writing in my notebook after shifts about the two of them.

Speaking of lost puppies, turns out Officer Shane and I were just meant to be friends. It's as if one day, I couldn't stop wanting him to be the answer and then on another day, well, it was done. I remember the day, too, when I knew that that desire had moved out of me. He showed up in the restaurant. "Honest to God, I was SURPRISED!" I reported to Shirley later that day. "Not only that, but I didn't feel no different than I had two seconds before layin' eyes on him. My heart didn't flutter; I didn't start sweating. None of it. I talked to him relaxed and plain as me. He told me he'd missed seeing me. Can you believe that? The nerve. But even that didn't get me. This shit works, Shirley!" I exclaimed.

I was in awe. I had known I was a loser, felt the gnaw of it for months, so invisible, all because he wasn't wanting to date me. Looking at him through my new eyes, I saw he was a bit too pale for my taste and his belly pooched out a bit.

"He's just a man, girl. Just a simple man. No super powers. Nothing," she said. "Well, it only took me ten notebooks full to figure that out," I thought.

I told her most of my conversation with Shane, how he'd wanted to talk about Danny's situation and then asked about Jim. Danny was going to be sentenced. Mama had been meeting with the lawyers; after that day at the jail, Danny hadn't wanted me involved. Shane, I'm sure, had details even Mama didn't know, but I didn't want to know what the lawyers or police said behind closed doors, and I told him as much. I'd spent more time worrying about her getting through it all, even though I was directed to let God take care of her. If anyone knew how to go to God for comfort, it was my mama. Maybe I was worse off about it than she was.

I didn't have it in me to tell him how I was handling Jim's death. Was a lot to tell somebody in a restaurant in the middle of a shift. Shirley confirmed my own thoughts. She told me that before I'd wanted something from Shane: a connection, comfort, intimacy. And now, well, "You don't," she said, "So why get into it? Why share those things?"

That woman was so wise as to how to help me understand what was coming to pass in my life. She made it clear many times that she was simply passing along what had been shared with her, but I suspected she put it into words just for me. She had a way about her, a gentleness and a directness that I could hear. She was safe.

She also told me I was entering the emotional process. "Good emotions. Full heart. You've worked hard, Charlie. Been willing." She assured me it was good and precious and to be in it as long as possible. "Plus," she said, "Makes you look like a saint."

And then she'd laugh her hearty laugh. "Just don't go thinking you're completely cured now. A daily reprieve is what we got. Put some of those days together. Feels good!" I assured her I hadn't gotten any such fancy ideas, but that I was learning a lot. I had to look up the word, "reprieve," which basically means the same as the word, "whew."

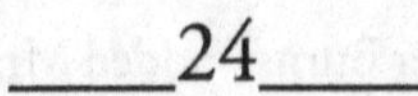

24

After some time of doodling with the charcoals and paper Mrs. Gillian had set me up with, I got the nerve to stop by her store and ask about going to her art class on Tuesday nights. "Of course, dear," was her reply.

Mama had insisted I bring the ginger snaps she'd baked. "It's only proper," she said. I argued with that woman as little as I could help those days and took the plate of cookies along with my art supplies.

I arrived at an old white farm house with red trim and a big wraparound porch. Her house was close to town. In fact, it was just down the street from the Bethel Lutheran where my women's meeting was. "Come on in, darlin'," Mrs. Gillian greeted me. "You're right on time." She took me into her kitchen, which was painted bright yellow and smelled of fresh lavender. She asked what I wanted to drink.

"Tea?" I said seeing a clear pitcher on the counter. "And I brought these," handing her the plate of cookies.

"Why, thank you," she replied pouring me a glass. "Everyone! This here's Charlie Montgomery. She's gonna be joining us tonight. She brought cookies!"

Right then from the adjoining room, which had a round table in the middle, a number of mis-matched chairs, and a peachy, floral couch, one of the other folks that had come responded, "I'm Ned!" And this skinny man about sixty years old introduced himself before grabbing one of the gingersnaps.

"He likes to get naked," Mrs. Gillian whispered to me.

"I've been known to on warm holidays," he joked back, smiling at her. I hoped that it wasn't going to be warm in Mrs. Gillian's house. From behind Ned stood up another old woman from the couch.

"And I'm Diane. Ned's wife. And don't worry. He's harmless." She elbowed him in the arm as he wrapped his around her and kissed her temple. Then the line of introductions began.

"Younger Burns and older Burns," added Mrs. Gillian. I had never heard the name "Burns" before and yet there was two of them.

"I've had time to have more sex," said older Burns, winking. Mrs. Gillian laughed when he said that.

"What kind of art class what this going to be," I thought. Then a gentle-eyed man about younger Burns' age, I was guessing early forties, though me guessing age was nothing but a piss-poor attempt, introduced himself as Benjamin.

Next was Ginger, who was a different redhead than Dakota. Where Dakota's hair was orangey, hers was a deep, deep auburn. I had never seen hair so silky and full in my life. Where Dakota was a stick, this woman was not. She was curvy all over. Her voice was soft and husky. She offered me the seat next to her. I had the feeling right away that we would be friends.

The woman Justine was the most mysterious, saying the quietest "Hello," but I guessed there was always one in every group. I decided I wasn't going to let her standoffishness bother me too much.

I was having a hard enough time believing I was there. I had no idea what was going to come next but there wasn't much art happening. We spent a good forty-five minutes gabbing away, shooting the shit. The Burns were musicians on top of being good at drawing. "Accomplished," Mrs. Gillian informed me. Turned out they were scheduled to play on the Square early March, and suggested we all should go. I hoped I wasn't scheduled to work. I found everybody so interesting, like I'd stepped into a vision of my life I hadn't known I'd been allowed to have.

In the middle of Ned talking about one of his most memorable naked adventures, the door swung open and in walked a guy tall enough that his head blocked the hall light. When he stepped into the kitchen where I was, I saw his eyes were hazel, the kind that made them almost golden. He looked to be closer to my age with sandy blond hair, a little shaggy.

I felt dizzy. I started sweating as if I'd been standing in a shadeless parking lot mid-August. He stuck out his hand and introduced himself, "Dylan," he said, looking me straight in the eye.

"Charlene Louise," I said, before realizing I had spouted my full name like my mama would do.

"We call her Charlie," Mrs. Gillian added, helping to bring me back to my own two feet.

He moved past me, greeting everyone, and fixed himself a glass of tea. His shoulders were broad, his hips narrow and his legs long. Dylan was easy with folks. Every now and then he glanced over at me. I caught his eye once, and he smiled. That is when Mrs. Gillian decided it was time to actually do some drawing and called out, "Let's get to it!"

We followed her to the front of the house, as if she were walking us out the front door. That led us into a wide, open room that was her living room. All set up were chairs that looked like small benches forming a circle. In a corner she had poster-size, clip board-like things stacked that were to hold our pads of paper. In the center of the room was a table with an assortment of rusty hand-held gardening tools.

From that first five minutes of sitting on my bench, looking at my blank sheet of paper, I got to it. I looked at the shapes of the tools, the spikes and flat surfaces. I held the pencil loosely, so that the point was angled to the paper. Maybe drawing was like riding a bike. Time flew by. When Mrs. Gillian called the hour, I had forgotten there were ten other people in the room, even Dylan, whom I'd wind up thinking plenty about later.

I had smeared pencil on my finger and thumb and the resting pad of my hand and asked for the bathroom. I looked at myself in the antique, oval bathroom mirror. The light was dim in there, but my eyes were brighter than usual.

I came out of the bathroom as everyone was making their way out and saying their goodbye's. I decided that I was definitely going to go back to art night. Ginger shook my hand and gave me a sweet smile, as did the others. Not Ned. "I'm a hugger," he said as he wrapped his skinny arms around me and gave me a bony squeeze.

"Again, he's harmless," added his wife as she winked. Dylan was last to shake my hand standing under the porch light as a new moon slit the night behind us. "Pleasure meeting you, Charlene Louise."

"Likewise," I replied, wondering what genteel lady had stepped into my shoes to use manners that would make my mama beam. Dylan walked down the steps and headed down the street, looking back and giving a last little wave. I turned to Mrs. Gillian, "Thank you for having me."

"You're more than welcome, my dear. Come back next Tuesday."

"Oh, I'm gonna," I said as the lady in me must have left already. I was on cloud nine driving back to Mama's. I kept running the events of the night through my mind: meeting everyone, the zest they all seemed to have (except for Justine) and of course, Dylan's face. I took pleasure in remembering his hand in mine, his eyes before me, his straight white smile, and his lips.

When I got home and looked over the drawings I'd made, I could see the trowel, mini fork and hoe in an overlapping pile on my pages. I was impressed but not enough to share them with Mama. Her take on art wasn't the same as her take on sin but since it had nowhere near the practicality of knitting or baking, she paid it little mind. It could be a hobby, but best not take it too seriously. If an activity wasn't going to benefit a man, like a fresh-baked pie to fill his belly, or benefit a child, like a long afghan to wrap up a cold babe, then it was wasted adoration. I thought if I could work art in there somehow with loving Jesus, she might take to it differently, and only then would I show her how good I was—depending on how I progressed.

I went to bed that night feeling peaceful and happy like I hadn't in some time. It was different from being dog tired being on my feet ten hours straight at the restaurant or the exhaustion after a full cry. Was I experiencing the usefulness, the purposefulness Shirley and the others had told me about? It was strange to me, the way I felt, but I wasn't going to complain. It was good, I knew that much. I had the sense that my new God was involved. And I decided that this new God was just plain weird and something I'd probably never fully wrap my head around.

§

Turns out, I didn't have to think hard about drawing. I didn't have to talk myself into doing it and started doing a little every day. "Like building up a muscle," Shirley said.

What was coming out of me was more than rakes and hoes and toilet paper. "Look," I pointed to the pad I'd brought over to her house after work.

She looked hard over my sketches. "Wow. Now that's somethin,'" she said. I knew Shirley would get it. "Is that the Wild Woman?" she asked in a serious tone.

"It is!" I said half believing it myself. "Is it too strange?" She assured me it wasn't one bit. With me being new at the art stuff, I was afraid of turning into some flaky hippie girl who might stop shaving her armpits and who Mama would change her mind about.

"Now that ain't gonna happen, honey," Shirley replied. "You're just giving your spirit a chance to express herself is all. Nothin' to worry about. In fact, it's quite beautiful."

As she was talking to me, I saw my face in the hanging mirror in the hallway behind her and could see light reflected in my eyes. It was still there, like I'd seen at Mrs. Gillian's. Finally, Shirley said, "You gotta start practicing accepting a compliment." And she reached out and touched my shoulder.

"Suppose I gotta work on that. Thank you," I replied.

25

I was about overwhelmed with the good I was experiencing, as it didn't sit too right with my history. Of course there were exceptions, like the fact that my brother was locked up. And then there was the nastiness of working with Maryl and Ty in the kitchen.

That Thursday, I was working lunch and got yelled at by Maryl, as if she owned the whole fucking restaurant. She didn't, I had the mind to tell her, but instead I picked up the melted tuna plate and BLT on dry toast and turned without giving her another minute of my time. Turns out she didn't appreciate it, and I got cornered outside at the end of the shift while I was smoking me a cigarette before going back in to mop.

"I don't like your attitude walking off like that when I was talking to you," she started in on me. Her sidekick Ty, in his hateful way, stood beside her practically growling at me. "We bust our ass back there and when you let the damn food get cold, we gotta make it over. We ain't got no time for that," she kept on at me.

I stood there holding my cigarette, my hand steady, not blinking, my insides roaring. I'd been talked down to plenty in my lifetime, and it was coming to an end for me. She went on, "You know, Lenore don't like it, neither." Ty kept nodding, his face scrunched up. "But what I really don't appreciate is the attitude."

Well, there's only so much a person can take, I found out. She was so full of shit. I knew goddamn well Lenore loved me working there. And my attitude couldn't be better. I took as long a drag off my cigarette as I could, dropped it to the ground and took a step towards her. I was inches away from her when it dawned on me just how much taller I was than her.

I looked down my nose and with my finger in her face hissed, "Who the fuck do you think you are?" as the rest of my body shook so hard I thought I was going to have a seizure. "Don't you ever fucking talk to me like that again. You best get off my ass." I must have made my point, because Ty didn't move and neither did she.

I turned to head back inside. I didn't care what she would have done. I was ready to put my hands around her neck and squeeze the last of her ugliness out of her. Dakota was standing at the door as if she'd seen the stars rearrange themselves on one of her astrology charts. She moved out of my way and followed me inside to help finish closing for the day.

§

Later that night, I shared the events at my meeting. I wasn't angry about it anymore. I didn't feel good or bad about what had happened. Nobody scolded me, neither, for saying such horrible things. In fact, Willow asked me to lead us out in the Lord's Prayer.

I hung around outside for a short while talking with Shirley, Willow, and Elizabeth Ann. Elizabeth Ann had gotten to telling us about one of the students in her accounting class at State University. Said that the girl had gotten her car stuck on the railroad tracks one night, late. The tracks were up a grass hill away from the road on one side, but just above another road on the other side. The girl was obviously drunk. She went on to tell us that she had read about it in the paper that Sunday and then Monday morning greeted the poor girl with a smug remark in front of the whole class that she later regretted.

"Now if somebody's gonna do something that foolish, they ought to get called out," was Willow's take. I was surprised that Elizabeth Ann was ever able to stand in front of a whole room of people and talk to begin with, much less give someone a hard time. She must have been a different person altogether when she wasn't dealing with her home life, I decided.

"I still regret it, shaming that poor, dumb girl," Elizabeth Ann then giggled. "Thank goodness none of my foolish choices put my name in the paper," she added.

"Here, here!" Shirley chimed in.

"She endangered lots of people, driving drunk like that. I have no tolerance for it," Willow said. "Tell 'em the rest of the story. I've heard it before," she insisted.

"Well," Elizabeth Ann went on, "a train came along and couldn't stop in time. Yeah. The train plowed right into that girl's car. Knocked it off the tracks a hundred feet away. Was flat as a pancake. They had a picture of it in the paper. Was a Honda, I think."

We all stood around taken in by her story. The air was cool, but refreshing and crisp. She went on, "The tracks are on a hill, you see. She could've hurt or even killed people if it'd gone over the other side. And the train had to stop and all that mess." It did make me wonder about people who went to college. I couldn't dare ask. I didn't even have my diploma then, so to my way of thinking, I wasn't going to have to worry about it.

"Yeah, you did the right thing," Willow insisted, patting Elizabeth Ann's arm. And then she turned to me and said, "And you. Well, good on you for today," and she smiled her big, contagious smile. "We've been pushed around long enough."

"Here, here!" said Shirley.

§

As usual, I was wiped out when I got home. I went straight to bed. I fell asleep quickly but another dream woke me up. In it, I'd seen Jim. He was covered in muck from the bottom of the lake he'd drowned in. He didn't look scary to me: his eyes were clear, and he was trying to tell me something. I was barefoot at the edge of the woods and could hear the water lapping at my feet. I don't remember feeling cold, but I could see my breath.

Jim was a ways down from where I was standing, his mouth opening and closing. The moon was full above us. I bent down and picked up a stone perfectly round and skipped it across the lake. I watched it bounce three times. I'd never been able to skip a rock like that. Danny liked to make fun of me for it when we were little, as if it was another important talent I lacked.

"Look at that!" I shouted in the dream, as the rock plunked into the water after the last skip. I turned back to look at where Jim had been standing but he was gone.

I called Shirley before work and told her I had a new one. She said it was all right for me to stop by after, and I could stay for supper, which I did.

After we ate, George left us in the kitchen while he went out back to his workshop to "twiddle with his tools and smoke his pipe," Shirley said. I helped her wash up and then sat down at the sturdy, oak table that had become familiar, comforting. I read her my dream.

"That's something, huh?" she said. I had been eager all day to hear what she'd think about it and that little "huh" wasn't giving me much.

"Am I losing my mind?"

"Girl, no. That's wild but you're not as out there as you think." She winked. "Looks like you're still working through Jim's death, honey. Interesting he didn't say anything in this one."

I nodded. We sat quiet for a moment until I told her how I'd never skipped a rock like that before. "Never in my life. Danny use to make fun of me. Couldn't throw no ball, skip no rock, though I could run all right."

She reminded me what she thought about dreams, how they were best interpreted by the dreamer. "We have our own symbols. It's a language just for us." She said she could tell me a thing or two, but it was more for my insides to really get. "I will say this, Charlie. You're doing all right. In fact, you're doing better than all right."

§

I was glad to hear what Shirley had said about my latest dream, because soon after Jim had accidentally drowned, the dreams had come almost nightly. The early ones were so disturbing I was scared to go to sleep, and if it hadn't been for my body being so spent from waiting tables, I'd have never rested. "Work is a blessing," Willow had gently reminded me.

I knew, well had been told, that grief could last a long time. It didn't matter whether it was a good relationship or not. He was my husband, my every waking thought for years. When I wound up in the hospital that last time, it was like the cord from me to him had been frayed. I had no way of knowing that I wouldn't be bound to the loss forever.

When I got home from Shirley's, I wrote some more on my dream about Jim and how no words came out of his mouth. "Maybe he doesn't got nothing to tell me no more," I scribbled in my child's scratch for handwriting in my spiral notebook. Sitting on the bed, I pulled my knees to my chest, my back against a set of pillows, and the blanket in a small fort around my feet. Despite all my crazy, I could see how I'd been set free. Sounds like a bunch of la-la bullshit to say, but that is what I came to know.

Then there was me skipping that rock. Something about that made me happy. Three full skips and a plunk. I couldn't wait to go to art class after that. I wrote that down, too.

26

It was late Sunday afternoon. The weekend had turned out long and boring. It rained the whole time and the weather was still cold enough as we were at the tail end of February. Lenore's had been slow over the last few days. I was getting restless, which made me smoke more which made my cough worse. I wandered into the kitchen.

"Those things are working the will of the Devil, Charlene Louise," my mama said after a gnarly coughing fit.

"Oh, Mama. I can't see the Devil being in cahoots with tobacco," I said while getting me some water.

"Anything that takes you from God is of the Devil," she replied, convinced.

"Okay, Mama," I said trying to get her to leave it alone. I'd given up everything else. No man, no pot, and no booze. "I'm practically living the life of a nun."

She didn't pay my rambles of self-pity no mind. She went back to focusing on her current project. Mama made quilts in the spring and summer, and she was getting prepared. She gathered clippings of cloth from the wholesale fabric store off Highway 81 near Parksville, about two towns north. She had hers spread like puzzle pieces across the table.

Before I walked out of the kitchen, she asked when I'd like to visit Danny. Pastor Eppleby had taken Mama a number of times, and maybe it was time I took her. The thing was, I couldn't imagine Danny being any different in County than he had been at the time of his arrest. Mama had said he was cleaned up and had gained some weight. I didn't know if I could count on her to tell me the truth about him and his state. I didn't know that I'd have the strength to see him. His emptiness had been eerie, like a dark wind blowing through a broken window.

Shirley said that it was possible he was still "sick" and that I didn't have to put myself through that if I didn't want to. In fact, she said it may be better if I didn't go until I got stronger, especially after Jim's death.

She was right. Seeing my brother next to dead made me feel helpless. I felt like I'd been lucky and had gone and broke some wicked spell. I was afraid Danny was like Candy and the rest of the women that came in and out of our survivors' meeting but didn't stay. I didn't know why I had surrendered to another way of living, with me being as stubborn as I was.

But then, looking at Mama bent over the table, her eyes squinted tight while she moved pieces of cloth around, I felt like I'd do anything she wanted me to. "When you wanna go, Mama?" I'd recommit myself to Jesus if she would have asked me right then. I would drive her in the pouring rain to get to my brother right that minute if she looked up at me and said, "Now, Charlene Louise. I want to see my son now."

My mama's lips still had color on the rims from church that morning. She opened her mouth and then closed it before a sound came out. Almost like Jim in my dream. She rested her hands on a piece of cloth with a navy background and bright yellow sunflowers. "How about next Saturday? Do you work next Saturday?"

I couldn't tell her that I'd need to take off. She would never let me do that. "Yes, Mama. That will be all right." Her hands started moving again, and she was back to the swatches before her.

I went to the back porch, to my Daddy's old chair where I'd left my sketch pad and a new charcoal pencil I bought. I sat down and started drawing. I must have looked like Mama had at her kitchen table before her pieces of fabric. I became lost in it.

27

It had been a long day at work, as early March was beginning to bring tourists into Eden's Gap, being near the mountains that was also a national forest. I'm sure Lenore appreciated business picking up again. But I'd lived in the country my whole life and didn't see what the thrill was in wandering around in the woods.

Once in my car, my body stiff and achy, I didn't know how I was going make it home and back out to art class. I pulled up to Mama's and was surprised to see her on the front porch. She was sitting in one of her old rocking chairs. That one had belonged to her mama.

She was rocking slowly and stopped when I pulled up. "You all right, Mama?" I asked, a little nervous as to what she might say. She didn't look like she had anything to keep her hands busy on her lap, so they lay still on top of the blanket wrapped across her knees.

"Such a nice afternoon," she answered starting to get up. "Made us some supper." She was moving slower than usual. This, too, made me wonder.

"Mama. I asked if you were feeling okay." I went to the side of her and reached my hand under one of her elbows to help her up. Once on her feet, she turned to me.

"Of course, Charlene. Why wouldn't I be?" she replied without shaking off my light hold.

"I just never seen you sittin' out here's all."

"I's havin' me a little talk with Jesus."

"Well? What's Jesus got to say?" She turned and looked at me. There was yellow light coming from inside the hallway through the windows in the front door, so I saw her blue eyes sparkle. She let out half a chuckle before covering her mouth with a hanky. I hadn't seen where she'd been keeping it, but out it came soon as needed.

She moved past me to the front door to go in. I could hear her muffling more giggles as I followed her.

"What?" I asked, not quite sure if she was laughing at my question or at something Jesus may have actually said to her.

"Charlene Louise," she said finally. "You should talk to him sometime. He'll listen."

I was relieved they'd had a good talk, that nothing was wrong. "I have to wash up before we eat. Then I'll come help you."

I could smell that Mama had fried up some chicken, so I hurried to kick off my shoes by my bedroom door, get out of my work shirt and get to washing my face. As I did, I was thinking about how seeing my mama like that was special. She'd always been so focused on preparing something, repairing something, or correcting something to be much fun. The most excited I'd seen her was when she and her church lady buddies gossiped about some poor soul. "Bless her heart. Bless his heart," they'd throw in to make it less of a sin.

"Let her have some fun," Danny used to say whenever I made a face over it. Whatever, was my feeling then. Now, I was grateful.

When I walked in the kitchen, the smell of the grease and seasonings made my mouth water. I saw that on the middle of the table sat a layered cake with chocolate frosting. "Happy Birthday, Charlene Louise," it said in yellow icing. "Oh, Mama..."

"Well," she replied, "Let's eat supper first, and then we can light the candles." I had forgotten it was my birthday but not my mama. We ate supper and had a piece of my cake. She'd sung, "Happy Birthday," and I saw a little tear in her eye. It warmed my heart. I helped her clean up, then out the door I went.

§

It wasn't until I pulled up to Mrs. Gillian's and saw the truck that I remembered I'd get to see Dylan. I hadn't done much to freshen up but turns out, I didn't care. I'd had a good day. Worked hard, spent time with my mama, and now was going spend time with my charcoals.

Dylan got out of his truck. "Hi there, Charlene Louise," he said as we walked up to the house together. Oh boy, a part of me liked him teasing me, because he seemed soft about it.

"That's right," I replied, "I don't answer to anything less." I could tell he was smiling in the dark. I just knew it.

He held the door open for me and followed me in. It looked like we had come together. I liked that idea just fine.

"Hello!" We got a fun-filled greeting from those inside already, which was most everybody. The place was lively and Ned started with hugs for us both. He squeezed me so tight I almost got a free back adjustment.

"Easy now. Don't go poppin' Charlie's eyes out," Mrs. Gillian said as she stood there waiting to hug me herself.

"Eight hugs a day! I was making mine worth at least half of the daily requirement," Ned joked. Mrs. Gillian told us to grab some tea and have a seat. Give us a chance to catch up on the latest, which we did. There was talk of Old and Young Burns playing music on the Square that Friday. Ginger and I talked about our weeks, me at the restaurant and her driving handicapped folks around to appointments and such. That was her job, and she seemed to like it from how she said she was "endeared" to some of her "clients." I had a hard enough time being patient to able-bodied folks at Lenore's, so I thought, "Bless your heart, Ginger."

I wasn't ready to share my piddly sketches of the Wild Woman with anybody from art class just yet. I had left them at home. That night the still life in the middle of our benches was of five different kinds of chairs arranged in what seemed like a dangerous pile. We were encouraged to walk around it to see the different perspectives before settling in on one.

It was my second night of art class and time passed like the first, slipping by me like a wet bar of soap. When the last hour was up, it was like coming out of a coma. I almost had to be reminded of where I was, like waking up in a different room.

I said the usual goodbyes and out on the porch, Dylan and I went together, like how we had come in. It worked out that way. I hadn't put effort into the arrangement, him and me. Sure, he was cute and seemed kind. And being next to him did raise my body temperature. But I was so taken in by the charcoal in my fingers and the movement of my hand over the paper, that any thoughts of him were like heated-up leftovers.

Dylan walked me to my car, telling me about working on his mama's house. I'd asked him where he lived and it seemed to light him up to talk about how he had recently moved in with his mama to restore the old windows. "It's quite a project, let me tell you," he said. She lived down the street and around the corner from Mrs. Gillian. That's how he had heard about "art night" since they were neighbors.

"I was coming from Amos's Lumber tonight. Otherwise, I'd have walked," he continued.

"Would have been a nice night for it," I thought. I had on my usual flannel button down over a t-shirt. The air was cool and fresh.

I fumbled around for my keys trying to hold my paper and bag of charcoals. "Lemme help with that," he said and his hand touched mine as I struggled to uncurl my fingers from the baggie. I felt a warm sensation in my chest.

"You got plans Friday night?" he asked as I was leaning over the backseat.

"Whaa?" I mumbled, pulling my head out. I looked him over, waiting for him to repeat what I thought he'd just said.

"Are you busy Friday night?" he repeated, his voice low and gentle. He was lulling me with the kindness in his face.

"What's Friday?" I clumsily asked him back.

"Music on the Square. It's this Friday night."

"Oh, that's right. They were talking about it when we walked in tonight." I must have let out a sigh.

"They're really good." He put one hand on my shoulder and said, "No pressure, Charlie. Come out if you can." He kept his gaze locked on me saying, "Hope you will."

Despite feeling the awkwardness like that of a newborn calf or colt with those skinny legs trying to raise them up to stand the first time, I managed a smile. I told him I'd try to come out, knowing I would, God help me.

28

When I got home, Mama had her bedroom door closed and no light was coming out beneath the door. Not having to talk let me stay in the fantasies I'd been creating on my drive up the mountain. I didn't go so far as to think about what our house would look like, but I did imagine meeting Dylan's mama for the first time. Would she like me? How was she going to feel knowing that I had been married before and that my husband had been in the paper for his accidental drowning, and that my brother was in prison and had also been in the paper for armed robbery?

In the hallway, a light was on for me and there was a note on the table by the phone. In my mama's handwriting was Lenore's name and a phone number I didn't recognize. I was curious to know why she'd called and who that number was for.

Next morning, I woke up near 8:00 which was about like sleeping until noon to my mama. She'd done had her breakfast hours before and the coffee pot was cold. I made some fresh, poured a cup, and stepped out onto the porch to smoke.

My chest hurt. I was getting sick of smoking. Didn't know how I'd ever quit. Though Shirley never pushed it, she said she'd help when I was ready. I didn't feel there yet but my chest felt tight and I was starting to wake up congested. That and Mama giving me a hard time for all the tissue I used.

"I'm gonna quit soon," I told her as if working up the courage. Shirley told me that when I was ready to, I had best be ready to cry. Great, I thought. I've already spent years bawling my eyes out. What more did I have to cry about?

The morning was surprisingly warm out. I took off my sweatshirt and sat down on the same rocking chair Mama had sat in the night before. Maybe I'll try this rock 'n' chat she was telling me to try. I mean how different would it be from what Shirley was having me do already: Serenity Prayer and endless writing in my notebook?

"Dear Jesus or my new God," I started, feeling as if I was making a bad joke. No matter. I began my nonsense while watching the sun make light lines on the grass. I was talking out loud, too, but quiet enough, not wanting Mama to hear me.

"Could you do me a favor, Jesus/God?" I asked. "Could you let me know for sure that Dylan likes me before I start to really like him? Also, could you not let me be a dumbass around him so much? Also, could he really like me for real? Oh and Jesus, one last thing. Could you ask the Wild Woman to come back to me in a dream? I sure am dreaming a lot anyway. She could come back to me that way." Seems like that would be all right to mention, I thought.

I felt I needed her to guide me here on out. She was the one who started it all. I had been drawing her so much, but from a hazy memory. And honestly, I wanted her to tell me what to do next. I know I had Shirley. Nothing and nobody could replace Shirley. But this was different. There had to be more than me getting up and running out of a cave in the woods. There was something more for me.

I decided that I'd had a nice chat with the good Lord and that was that. I got up and went inside. Mama reminded me that I had a message from the night before. "Thanks, Mama. I'll call Lenore back right now," I said as I picked up the phone to dial her number.

Lenore picked up. "Glad you got my message. I wanted to see if you'd like to join us this Sunday at the Safe Depot," she asked in her direct way. She went on to tell me they had some new women at the house, and they could use folks to talk to. She added that she thought I might benefit by becoming involved. I had a sense that she and Shirley had concocted this plan on my behalf, them knowing each other.

I agreed. It was only for a couple of hours on Sunday. Willow would stop in and maybe Dakota. I'd see Dakota at work and ask if she wanted to go together.

I went ahead and asked off for Saturday, while I had Lenore on the phone. "My mama wants me to take her to see Danny. I haven't been in a while."

There wasn't a second of hesitation from her. "Of course. You be there for your family. Most important thing to do. We'll cover at the restaurant." I was relieved, since I'd already let on like I was off and didn't know how to tell Mama I couldn't go if that had been the case.

"Things seem all right, Shirley," I explained to her, my last phone call before work.

"Just keep putting one foot in front of the other, dear," she said. "I think it's great you're going to the Safe Depot this weekend, too. Gonna be a busy weekend for ya!" Then she laughed her big laugh, and I could just see her face with her serious eyes and wide smile lined in ruby red lipstick.

"Grateful to you," I said.

"I know, dear. I know," she replied before we hung up.

My weekend was going to be packed, not so boring like the last week. Friday night was music and seeing Dylan, Saturday was visiting Danny, and then Sunday was this Safe Depot meeting thing. It was only Wednesday, and I couldn't believe how full my life was getting. All this coming from a girl who spent years holed up in a trailer doing nothing but smoking weed and watching old movies and wishing for a different life.

I got ready for work. The drive down the mountain was beautiful. The trees were green and the sun was streaming through the leaves. I rolled the windows down, no radio, and listened to the wind instead. Part of my drive ran alongside a creek. It was full and running, and I could hear the water. I had never cared about shit like this. The air was wet and fresh and smelled clean, and I filled my lungs with it.

I pulled into work alongside Dakota. She was looking so much better. No bruises. No bags under her eyes. She had gotten an apartment in town by herself, which amazed me. Dakota never did come to my meetings but seemed to be fine living on her own. Cole was still a bastard. She had gotten a restraining order against him but told me she would let him over every now and then.

It didn't matter, she would say, because she loved having her own place to do "whatever the fuck she wanted." That's how she put it. "I can fart and not be treated like a servant in my own goddamn house."

I began to think about living on my own from all Dakota's talk about it. I didn't see how I could leave Mama, though. There wasn't a soul for miles from her house, her being out a ways. Plus, I liked Mama's company after all. And I was beginning to think that she liked mine enough.

As Dakota and I walked near the back entrance of Lenore's, she brought up the other day when I about went off on Maryl and Ty. "Girl, it was priceless, whatever you said. The look on her face...I was scared of ya when you walked in."

"Shut up!"

"No, seriously," she said. "Honest to God, I was."

"You're crazy," I teased her. "I dunno, Dakota," I said, "I don't know what happened. I just couldn't take their bullshit no more. Sick of the two of 'em. I didn't get out from Jim for that."

"I hear ya. I do. I knew you had some fire in your chart somewhere." She put her skinny-ass arm around my shoulder and squeezed me beside her. Then she let go and pushed me up ahead of her and gave out a big laugh, like Shirley had earlier on the phone. "You're tougher than people think, Charlie. You know that, right?"

"Yeah. So tough. I'm scared to sneeze most days."

"You ain't. Not no more. That was the old Charlie. This here's somebody different. You're different than when I met you." She was talking to me from behind as we made our way in through the heavy, wooden back door.

"Hey," I turned around before going all the way in. "You going on Sunday or not? To the Safe Depot thing?" She said she would if I would. "I think I kind of have to," I said.

We made plans for me to pick her up. Dakota would tell me how to get there from her place, since she'd been before and she lived on the way. "You can see my new place," she added.

The day flew by. We were packed from 11:00 until 2:30. I never lost steam, and Maryl and Ty never said a word to me. They didn't give me a hint of attitude, neither. Yep, things were changing all around me.

29

Thursday night, while the ladies and me were standing outside after our meeting, I told them what Dakota had said about living on her own.

"The freedom to fart with dignity!" Willow hollered. "If that ain't motivation to get out."

Elizabeth Ann was red in the face but had tears in her eyes she was laughing so hard. She handed out tissues to the rest of us for our own.

I couldn't wait for Friday to roll around. And when it did, I couldn't wait for work to be over. I stopped by Kmart on the way home to get something new to wear. I hadn't been clothes shopping in decades. I hadn't changed much, weight-wise, over the years. Hallelujah. Waiting tables kept me moving plenty.

Dakota and I had talked about walking around the fields at the small college down the hill from town after work one of these days but had not done it. My feet were always too sore to think about more walking at the end of a shift.

"It would be good if we took our shoes off and stood in the creek," Dakota had suggested.

"Isn't it cold?" I replied. I thought she was nuts, us standing barefoot in the creek at the school in front of everybody who walked by like we were two hillbillies. Truth was I was embarrassed to go on a college campus not having finished high school. Dakota kept bringing it up.

"Fine," I gave in.

"When?" She was pushing it. I knew to just give in or she would keep nagging. I replied, "Whenever!" I just wanted to get through the weekend.

I stood in a short line holding my basket of items. I had picked out a hot pink shirt with a scooped neck, made of soft fabric. It draped over my shoulders. I had also picked some dangling silver earrings and a new lipstick, a lighter version of my pink shirt. And lastly, I threw in some perfume called "Exclamation", so I wouldn't have to smell like a granny. I had a lump in my stomach, the total nearly thirty bucks, but it had been a while since I had treated myself, I reasoned. I handed the cashier thirty-five dollars, and she handed me back my change.

§

"This is my new shirt," I showed Mama after showering and getting ready. "You like it?"

"Yes, Charlene. That's a nice blouse." All shirts were blouses to my mama. All pants were slacks and that was an exception to skirts, which she preferred. She was sad that I still wore jeans for what she was calling a date.

"It ain't a date, Mama. Just meeting some friends on the square."

"Well, be polite and be a lady," she instructed, as if I might slip into spitting chew and scratching my privates. Then I heard her mumble something about me not wearing a skirt, like a true lady...blah, blah, blah.

"Yes, Mama," I said while rolling my eyes. "You wanna come hear the music? You might like it. It'll be old-timey."

She declined but thanked me for asking. She was going to stay home, work on her quilt, and probably prepare herself, though she didn't say it to me, for visiting Danny tomorrow. I didn't feel like thinking about Danny at all and was happy to think about my night out instead.

§

I smoked close to five cigarettes on my short drive to town. I hadn't expected to get so worked up, but the reality was I never went out. I had asked Dakota to come, but she said she didn't like no bluegrass. These people were my other friends anyway. She wasn't interested in meeting a bunch of "old fogeys," as she put it. She did say she was dying to see what Dylan looked like. I hadn't told her too much about him, other than he was fine and sweet. The truth was that I didn't know that much about him. That was enough. Dakota said that with that combination, he sounded a bit like a unicorn.

I parked on a side street and walked up the short hill to Main Street. I sprayed a few pumps of the Exclamation before getting out of the car and hoped the walk would air me out from both cigarettes and my cover-up job. The air was mild and not humid. A perfect night.

Main Street had been blocked off for two blocks and there were people lined up in lawn chairs, kids running around, and a few couples dancing nearer to the stage where a group I didn't recognize was playing music. They looked closer to my age, a girl playing the fiddle and three guys playing bass, guitar and banjo.

Closer to the courthouse, I saw people I did recognize on the lawn in front. I saw Mrs. Gillian in a long skirt and sweater vest talking to Ned and his wife, Diane. Ned looked as if he could barely stand still, his one foot tapping away to the music. They greeted me as I walked over, between other families with blankets laid out on the grass.

I got hugs from everybody. I didn't see Dylan, which gave me a moment to collect my nerves. Not more than a minute, though, and I felt a gentle hand on my back and heard a voice that made me smile. "Hello, Miss Charlene Louise." I turned around.

"Well, hello, Mr. Dylan," I replied. He stood close enough that I could smell him, nice, like Irish Spring soap. I didn't want him to move. Everything in my body went light and relaxed. I looked up to him to see him grinning, his smile bright.

Dylan was wearing a blue jean shirt and a Carhartt ball cap. We stood side by side, my arm brushing the rolled up sleeve of his shirt, as he pointed out to me Young Burns and Old Burns over to the right side of the stage.

Ned piped up over the banjo music, "Nice job, Dylan, with the stage and the trellis over it."

"Thank you. Wasn't much to it. Not when you have good help," he replied. I had a surge of pride standing next to Dylan, the guy who built the stage.

"Well, it makes it nice for everybody. You have done a good job," assured Ned. His wife smiled silently beside him, nodding. Then in a blink, Ned shouted out, "Let's dance!" He pulled Diane to him and started swaying her back and forth to the music which was now a slow ballad.

"Want something to drink?" Dylan asked me. "I brought a cooler." I froze, realizing that I would have to explain that I wasn't drinking booze, that I didn't want to anymore. I was afraid that he would think I was uptight and no fun.

He pulled out a glass bottle of Coke and held it out to me. "Thirsty?" Relieved, I said yes. He unclipped his Swiss army knife set from his jeans and popped the top off and gave it to me. "Anyone else?"

Mrs. Gillian said she didn't drink real Coke anymore. Dylan popped one open for himself and chugged half of it. "Didn't realize I was so thirsty myself," he said as he wiped his mouth and stared at me as he waited for me to take a few sips before clinking bottles with me.

The music had stopped playing and Young Burns and Old Burns were setting up. They had a few guitars out and Young Burns had one of those harmonica metal chinrests around his neck. I was excited that I knew them and couldn't wait to hear them play with all that had been talked about the last couple of art nights.

While we stood there waiting, Dylan tilted his head towards me and asked me about myself. I didn't like this and wished the two Burns would get to playing. I told him that I was from Eden's Gap, well, up the mountain a bit. I told him that my Daddy had died a ways back and that my mama was doing all right and that I had a brother. Lord help me, as I did not know the meaning of light talk. He didn't ask about how my brother was doing, thank God. If he had, I'm sure I would have spilled, and I wanted him to think I was somewhat normal for as long as possible.

Dylan told me that his family was originally from Georgia. "Ever been to Elberton?" he asked. "Big place for granite." I hadn't been farther than down Highway 76, I told him.

He laughed but had an almost sad look on his face. "There's a big world out there, Charlie. We're stuck in a small part of it." The word "stuck" hit like an opened palm landing in middle of my chest. "You okay?" he asked while putting his arm around my shoulder, giving it a squeeze.

I absorbed his touch and took in a deep breath. That's when Young Burns started blowing on the harmonica and Old Burns began strumming his guitar and then they both belted the first lines of their first song in perfect harmony. If I'd had a flowy skirt on, I would have twirled it 'round and 'round.

They played, "Orange Blossom Special," "Blue Moon of Kentucky," "John Hardy," "Summertime," and "Rocky Top." Those were the songs I knew from my granny and Paw-Paw's, when Danny and I stayed with them. I clapped my heart out. The rest of the time the music was going, Dylan and me were side by side. It felt so natural to be there with him and Mrs. Gillian and the others. The stage was lit up bright. The crowd clapped and hollered each time Young Burns and Old Burns finished a song.

A few other singers and guitar, banjo, and fiddle players, in addition to the younger group, all I'd never seen before, had joined in for a song here and there before they stopped playing. Despite the night coming to an end, a "blessed be thy name" kind of night, I didn't have that sense of dread hovering over me. I wasn't thinking about when I wouldn't be seeing Dylan again.

He said he would walk me to my car, so we said our goodbyes to the others and started back down Main Street past the families packing up their blankets and chairs to head to their cars, too. I spotted a bright red blanket over the arm of a woman wearing a purple smock. She was standing in front of the coffee shop with another familiar face next to her.

"Shirley!" I called out, happy they would see me with Dylan. She did light up, as did Willow standing beside her.

"Well, hello," she replied. I introduced Dylan to both of them, and when he responded like a gentleman, I got a double look of approval. I told them he was walking me to my car and Shirley told me to call her tomorrow once I got back. "Doesn't matter how late it is, hon," she said.

"I appreciate it." Then we said our second round of goodbyes and headed on.

"Where you going tomorrow?" Dylan asked, not realizing what the answer would be and how the look on my face must have told him so. "I'm sorry," he said, "You don't have to say. None of my business."

"No, it's all right." I decided that I'd go for it. Tell him the truth. I went on to tell him how my brother was in jail and that I was going to take my mama to see him. I was less embarrassed than I thought I'd be, though his quiet pauses were right uncomfortable. He listened to me tell him how hard it was on my mama and how she was religious and so thought it was a lesson God was giving her, testing her faith. "That's her," I said and sighed.

"She sounds like a strong woman, Charlie." I didn't tell him how strong she really was given what she'd been through. That could come later, if there was a later with me and him. "You seem pretty strong, too," he said as he stopped us there on the street and held me.

I didn't question him, though I wondered how he'd come to that conclusion. Was it in the lines I drew in charcoal in the few nights of art class that gave away my secrets and how I'd come through? Was the Wild Woman coming out in me in ways I couldn't possibly see?

Shirley would tease me about becoming philosophical. I didn't even know what that word meant until she told me to look it up: "Investigation of the nature, causes, or principles of reality, knowledge, or values, based on logical reasoning rather than empirical methods." I didn't know what half those words meant, but I could guess they didn't sound like me, to me. But I took her word for it.

"When you're not busy trying to survive, you have time to ponder the deeper meaning in everyday events," she had said. "That's why you gotta continue to journal. Even that type of thinking can get overwhelming. Gotta stay present. Stay grounded, hon."

Dylan took my hand in his hand. He didn't try and kiss me, he just held my hand tenderly. It didn't feel like rejection, as Shane's hugs had. Dylan walked me to my car holding my hand the whole way. I was thinking I might fall for him. I didn't know if that was okay, given my history. Was it safe for me to fall in love ever again, even with somebody sweet and thoughtful in addition to being terribly handsome?

When we got to my car, he released my hand and held the door open for me to get in. "Good night, Charlie. I'm glad you came out." I gave a little wave as he stood there watching me drive off. I felt tingly all the way down to my shoes. I'd need to be, for the day ahead of me.

____30____

I was singing, the echoing rhythm of the old-timey songs playing in my head, as soon as I'd come to Saturday morning. It was early but light out. Mama was frying up bacon to go with the biscuits she had made yesterday. I jumped in the shower, though I liked thinking I could still smell Dylan, maybe on my hair. Nope. Smelled like smoke.

I took my biscuit wrapped in a paper napkin and a mug of black coffee in the car, though Mama complained that it wasn't safe to drive that way. "Mama, I eat, smoke, and drink in the car all the time. Before you know it, we'll be talking on the phone, too."

"Hmph," she responded, her hands clasping her purse in her lap. We weren't going to talk about Danny, so I talked too much about my night. "He seems to be a good one, Mama. Shirley was out. She met him."

"Does he attend church regular?" was her first question, which I should have known was coming.

"I can't say. Hasn't come up." She hmphed again. She was wearing a lavender straw hat, some fake flowers along the rim, like she would wear to church. It was going to be a beautiful spring day. Though early, I would have rolled down the windows and taken in fresh air, had Mama not been in the car with me. She wouldn't want her hat to fly off, or worse, her hair to blow.

I told her about the music and how they played songs she would know and like. "It was for everybody, Mama. Younguns were out with their parents and older folk, too."

Though she was generally worried about anything that wasn't dedicated to His holy name, she perked up when I mentioned "Orange Blossom Special." I started to think that maybe she hadn't always been on such a Jesus-strict diet.

It wasn't but a forty-five minute drive to the county jail, but we had to get out on the highway. That raised my spirits, as I could drive up to sixty or more, and I liked being alongside the eighteen-wheelers, the roar of their engines compared to the itty-bitty hum from our car. Then the rigs would be right on our tail on the downhill. Mama didn't like it one bit. She was sitting stiff as a board, eyes glued ahead of her. She would grasp the door handle when I'd speed up to pass anyone, as if she was going to jump out if it looked like we weren't going to make it.

"Mama, I have to get around 'em. Otherwise, we won't get there on time."

"No, you don't, Charlene. We left plenty early. All in God's time."

Mama took out the directions she had written down from her purse. She began to read them to me. We were to head down the road off the highway for about a mile and then turn left onto Raintree Drive. There were old mill houses along Raintree, kids playing in some of the yards, mostly patches of weeds and dirt. Those people lived their lives right down the road from the thick-walled yard of the jail.

We got through the gate, then the front entrance to the stone building. We signed in and waited. I spotted mounted cameras watching us from all corners outside and in. Mama was quiet the whole time. I wished for another smoke. I had sucked one down after parking, as I didn't know when the next one would be. I was there to be of service to my mama, I reminded myself, and that made my fears second, which in a strange way made it easier on me.

We were then led into a not much bigger than a closet sized room, painted a pukey yellow, and Danny was escorted in moments later by a large, ugly guard. The big man's face looked to be swollen and red, like he'd been stung by bees, but that was his face. He had a meanness about him I recognized. I didn't like the idea of him myself and wondered if they were all like that. Danny's hands were cuffed, as were his feet and he shuffled towards us slowly.

Danny then shocked the holy hell out of me because he smiled a wide grin at the both of us. Mama sat proper in her seat beside me. He looked Mama straight in the eye, then he looked at me. His eyes were clear. His hair cut short. He was clean. He had done accepted Jesus into his heart, so he told us. It had been recent, like within the past three weeks.

Mama was pleased as a peach in the Georgia sunshine. I had a hard time believing he was for real. I was skeptical, as three weeks is not that long, except that his eyes, well, something was different. I tried to liken it to when God had done for me what I couldn't do for myself, by way of getting Shirley and Mama and the law out interrupting me killing my husband. That I couldn't explain, but it was only the beginning and didn't make me less crazy overnight.

Danny threw out Bible verses and mentioned a guy named Frank who seemed to be his "Shirley." Frank was religious. I was glad Shirley wasn't. I don't think that would have worked for me.

Danny gave us a brief rundown about a meeting with his lawyer. He was going to plead guilty, and he would be going to prison. I heard Mama take in a breath. He worked to convince her that he was safe now and that he would be once sentenced. Danny said that he would write me.

"Good to see you, Charlie," he said.

"You, too," I said, though not whole-heartedly. I mean, what was this con he was pulling, acting like he was the man of the house again, that he loved us, and that was all that needed to be said? We were visiting him in jail. And hearing him spit out the Good Word as if all was forgiven so easy got stuck in my craw.

I made it through the next hour by gripping the hem of my shirt. If we weren't where we were, Mama would have scolded me for stretching it out. Maybe his new bullshit was better than him staring at the wall blankly while Mama and I fiddled with our fingers. Regardless, it hurt my head.

I was relieved when the ugly-faced guard showed back up to get Danny. Mama took out her hanky and wiped her eyes. She reached out a wrinkled hand and patted one of his. Nobody spoke the word "love," but that was her way of saying it.

In the car she muttered, "Praise Jesus," about a hundred times. I bet she couldn't wait to tell Pastor Eppleby and her church ladies. I remember thinking to tell her it might be better to wait to spread the good news, like waiting at least a few months before telling people you are pregnant. You know, in case something goes wrong early on.

I was glad that Mama seemed more relaxed, but all the way back, she had kept on and on about God's mysterious ways. I couldn't help it and let out, "He's full of it, Mama. More like Danny's workin' one over the good Lord, if you ask me."

"Nobody is askin' you. God's miracles don't need our time nor our understanding," Mama professed. I wanted to yell at her. Tell her she was a fool and believing him was only going to hurt us in the long run. But she was comforted. She was happy I took her to see him. I tried to talk myself into being thankful for that much. I could, I told myself. I was...and I was angry at the same time.

When Mama and I did get back to the house, it was around lunch time yet. But I was spent. The idea of picking up the phone was like it would have weighed a thousand pounds. I could not call Shirley like I had promised. I didn't have the energy to do much but heat up some leftover chicken and green beans, eat and take a shower and a long nap. I needed to wash off the yuck of the jail and the religious hoopla from my brother.

I shouldn't be surprised by then but when I woke up from my afternoon snooze, I remembered clearly a dream. I was staring down a hole in the floorboard at the end of my bed. It was like somebody had sawed a round circle and hung a light down in the space beneath. There was a rope dropped into it. I was on my hands and knees bent over the hole looking to see what was in there.

"Hello!" I called out. From a side shadow, Danny stepped out into the light. I saw his face. He looked up at me and smiled. That was it. I made note of it, scribbling it all down and went out to the back porch to sketch the rest of the night.

§

Next morning, I squeezed in a smoke before getting ready. There was a mist hanging over the trees, holding a damp blanket around the house. I had another full day of unexpected ahead of me. I gave Dakota a buzz letting her know I was on my way, also to make sure she was awake.

"You're a busy one now, aren't ya?" Mama said as I walked into the kitchen, took another biscuit and more coffee and headed down the hall toward the front door.

"Yes, ma'am. These days I seem to be." I didn't know how long I would be gone so told her not to wait for me for supper. She would be at church most of the day anyway, she told me.

I got to Dakota's apartment about a quarter to nine. She invited me in, got me some more coffee, and showed me around the place. Her apartment was nice, freshly painted a peachy-tan color. She had a full kitchen, with a dishwasher and a bar that opened to the dining room/living room area. She had a table and four chairs with place mats set all ready for company. In the middle was fake fruit in a moss-colored glass bowl. I felt a tinge of jealousy.

"Housewarming present from Lenore," she explained. I hadn't even thought of bringing her anything. Mama would have been ashamed had she known I was going to my friend's new place without bringing a gift. I wondered if it counted if I brought it later.

We walked down a short hall with a closet on one side that opened to a washer and dryer. Across from that was a bathroom that was bigger than

179

any in our house. And at the end of the hall was her bedroom. She had a full bed and a dresser, and her curtains matched her bedding. They were white with pale yellow dots. Dakota's bed had turquoise "accent" pillows, as she called them.

"Girl, this all came from that Home Again store on Mason Street," she told me. Dakota had up and left her boyfriend and left their furniture with him. "I didn't want none of that crap. Don't want to have his stuff in my new place. No thanks."

"Well, this sure is nice," I told her, no matter that it was used. I wouldn't have known if she hadn't told me anyway. "Real nice," I said again, envious as hell.

"Thanks, girl." She got us a glass ashtray, the ones heavy enough to break a window. We sat in her living room and smoked. She talked on and on about Mercury turning direct, which was good for her. "Mercury's all about communication. Makes things less scattered, girl."

I told her about visiting Danny and how he'd gone religious. "At least for the time being," I added.

"You don't believe him?"

"Seems too quick to me. I mean, what? It's been a few weeks? Maybe a month?"

"Yeah, I wouldn't be so sure either if I was you. I don't trust it when a person says they've changed overnight. Cole tried to pull that born-again bullshit on me, too. Puh-lease. It only made him meaner 'cause it made him feel guiltier about himself that he couldn't stay right."

"Aren't we sorry?" I teased her and me.

"You got that right."

"Well, at least you got you a fine place now," I said. She got up and emptied the ashtray, and I followed so we could head on to the Safe Depot for a full day of God knows what.

§

We had turned down a narrow dirt drive that was on the backside of a neighborhood not too far out of town. Lenore met us at the door. It was weird seeing her outside of the restaurant. "Come on in, girls, and meet some of our new guests."

I followed Dakota, who seemed braver than me. "I lived here for a short while, remember?" she assured me.

"Well, I lived in the hospital a short while. I'll lead us, then, we ever need to go there." We laughed quiet as we could before Lenore introduced us to the room, which was about three ladies. One was a tiny black lady who sat in a recliner on the far side of the living room. She didn't look up.

Lenore said the other guests were either upstairs or out—ten total. "That's about capacity," she let us know. Then she called out to the lady in the recliner, "Mary, this here's Charlie. You two might have a thing or two in common." Mary looked up from staring at her hands, and I saw one of her eyes swollen and bruised. Back in time I went.

31

I didn't have to work Monday, which kind of bummed me out since I hadn't worked all weekend. That was three days in a row of no pay. I had been trying to save a little when I could.

"You're not always gonna live with your mama, dear," Shirley reminded me often. "You'll have your own place soon. Good to get into the habit of paying bills and such." Just like Dakota, I thought. If she could do it, then maybe I could, too.

Since I had the day off, I made plans to spend the afternoon with Shirley. I was helping her clean out a couple of closets and rambled away. George was off having his weekly banjo lesson, so I could talk loud and we weren't stuck in the kitchen. Not that that was bad, but it was more fun to have Shirley not worrying about him walking in needing something. She would share more personal stuff when he was out of the house.

"You're not gonna believe what he did this time…" she'd start. "He farted so loud last night that I woke up from a dead sleep thinking there was gunfire in our room. He barely rustled. Just rolled over. I about peed myself. Didn't have the heart to tell him this morning." Telling me made her laugh again so hard she could barely catch her breath. "It's those moments that make him more special to me, Charlie."

I must have had a look on my face, because she said I would meet somebody one day where that would be true. "It's not like the past. Nope. Real love is different, dear. There isn't any shame in it."

I caught Shirley up on what she called "current events": Dylan, which was a sweet thought; visiting Danny and my weird feelings about that; there was Dakota's apartment; and then there was the Safe Depot and meeting the women in it like Mary with her busted-up eye.

"You can invite anyone of those women to the meeting, you know," Shirley put out there. Lenore had mentioned that to me, but since Dakota had stayed at the house and never went to a meeting, I didn't know if it was necessary. "It can't hurt," Shirley added.

I asked her how she knew if a person even wants to go. "Well, you don't know unless you ask. You can't worry about it if they aren't interested. Just put it out there." I didn't like that idea too much. "It's not about you, dear," she made clear.

Shirley could say things like that and it didn't hurt my feelings. And sometimes it wasn't until later when it'd make sense. In this case, she was saying my job was to put it out there. God's job was to worry about the why or why not. Looks like it had little to do with me long as I did my part, the right thing as best I knew it to be.

This took us to the part where I was annoyed with Danny acting all religious, as if he'd found Jesus into his heart and that was that.

"Like there's no more work for him to do. He sat there and spat out psalms this and that, not having nothing to do but hang out in jail and let the rest of the world work and not even seem to notice how he'd be gone away anyway," was how I was going on and on.

Shirley let me until I was finished. She was busy standing on a stool in her bedroom, reaching to bring down old shoe boxes. She handed them to me and I put them on the bed. She then stepped down a second and looked at me and said, "Do you think you might be mad at him for going about his life, as it was, and leaving you to marry Jim?"

"What do you mean?" I asked.

"Charlie, is it your brother's fault that you married Jim?" she asked, giving me her full attention. I wanted to respond but nothing seemed right to say. I started crying. She reached out, took me in her arms. "Yeah, I think we do blame the ones we love. It's all right, dear. It's all right."

I continued my crying, her hugging me made it seem okay. She smelled like rose petals. I let go and she found some Kleenex. "Shit," I said, wiping my eyes. "He was a good man. And he left. He should have been protecting me and Mama."

"I understand, hon. But he was a kid, too. Looks like you got some more writing to do." The thought of more writing was like she'd given me weights to hold in my hands, bringing my shoulders down. I know that wasn't the point. It was to help, but hadn't I covered that one a while back? I thought. I must have. How could I have missed that? Seems like it would have been in there with Daddy dying, except I felt that was a good thing, and then Jim dying which brought up a bunch of "unresolved anger," as Shirley had called it.

"Like peeling the layers of an onion. It's a practice," she said, as if it was a reassuring thing to say. I stood there, as if the blood in my body had stopped flowing. Weird thing about moments like that—and I'd had many with Shirley, in the meetings with the other ladies, and by myself—is that they seem too much to take until they pass. And they do pass. Sometimes I need people to remind me, but they do pass. Shirley said that's when the Wild Woman is free. That Shirley is woo-woo but she didn't scare me because I've experienced what she said to be the truth. Over and over again.

I let out a long sigh, shifted weight knowing I'd feel better soon, like more things in life are possible. It happens that way after one of them hidden feelings comes up. "Still got to write on it," she teased me.

Shirley got back on the step stool and pulled a few more boxes down. "Can you believe we got so much tucked away in here?" She then asked me to help her take them to her car. "Now, tell me about this Dylan fella. He seems like he might be all right, huh?"

"Oh my gosh! I had a great time Friday night. Dylan was so sweet. The music was sweet. It was weird and not weird at the same time," I told her.

"He does seem to have good energy, hon," was her response.

"I gave him my number. But I don't think I am too worried about him not calling me."

"Well, you had a lot going on this weekend. That's a good thing," she said. Then Shirley had me follow her to the hall closet after loading boxes of old shoes into the trunk of her car. I couldn't believe she had so much stuff she wanted to get rid of. "It's good to clean out the old. Make room for the new."

"I don't think my mama knows about this," I said. "My daddy's chair is still sitting on the back porch facing his old TV. She's still got a closet full of his clothes, too." She agreed that it might not be a task my mama would want to take on.

"But you can try it with your things. Old clothes. Perfect for new beginnings."

"Oh, my old clothes are comfortable—the way I like them," I told her.

"Nothing wrong with comfortable," she said. "Doesn't hurt to treat ourselves. Like that cute pink shirt you had on Friday night? Was that a treat?"

"It was. Though I wasn't sure it was okay to spend money on it. But I did."

"Good for you. You're working hard. You deserve color in your life!"

I didn't tell Shirley that all my socks, and panties for that matter, had holes in them. "Your task, should you be willing, is to make room for the new, is all," she said. "And gift yourself from time-to-time." I could do that much.

It was late afternoon by the time I left Shirley's. She had invited me to stay for supper, but I worried about wearing her out to the point she would never be able to hear me blab on and on and would no longer want to help me. She said I helped her as much as she helped me. She had been saying that from the beginning, though it was hard for me to believe. There was no way I could pay her back any way I looked at it.

"When you get home, why don't you ring up the Safe Depot? See how that woman, Mary, is doing," Shirley suggested.

I didn't know how long Mary would be in there; she could have left already. No matter. I just needed to check on her, to see if she wanted to come to a meeting with me. The rest wasn't up to me. "All right then, Mrs. Mary," I thought, "I'll check on you when I get home.

§

When I looked over the pad by the phone for messages, I had one from Dylan. Mama had written it down, meaning she must have talked to him. Oh Lord.

"Mama!" I called down the hall. I headed toward the kitchen. She looked up from her quilting, WROC quietly playing her religious favorites. "What did you say?" I asked her right off.

"Who, Charlene Louise, are you referrin' to?"

"You talked to Dylan, Mama. You wrote down that he called."

"Why, yes. Yes, I did. Sounds like a nice fella," she said returning to her needle and thread, patches of fabric clinging together draped across the table, a bag full of loose fabric by her side.

"And?" I asked her, my voice raised, which I instantly realized she wasn't going to like. "I'm sorry. What did he say?"

"Well, he asked to speak to you, of course. I told him you weren't here and would he like to leave a message."

"That was all?"

"Why of course. What else would there be to say?" she replied.

Oh, I don't know, Mama, I thought. How about "Charlene Louise was married not too long ago. Her husband died a tragic, sad death." Or "My son has found Jesus. Have you? Have you accepted Jesus as your Lord and Savior?"

I called Dylan back first rather than calling Mrs. Mary at the Safe Depot, although I suspected I should have done it the other way around.

He wanted me to know that he'd had a good time Friday night. "I did, too," I told him. We talked a minute about the music and then seeing each other at Mrs. Gillian's.

Then I called the Safe Depot. A woman I didn't know, who said her name was Brenda, answered. "I was there yesterday," I explained, "Lenore had invited me to come by. I'm a survivor, too." Had I ever said those words out loud before? I didn't think I had but they fit me like my skin.

"Oh, I must have been out. At work," she explained. "Let me see if she can come to the phone."

"Hello," Mary's soft, hesitant voice answered. I went into the whole deal reminding her who I was and why I was calling. I explained how I went to a women's meeting on Thursday nights and how it helped me.

"Uh-huh," was all she said in return.

"So, I was wondering if you'd wanna go with me this week. I'd pick you up."

"Uh-huh. Well, I gotta think about it. You see, I might not stay here that long. Might have to go home, you see." I remembered how Shirley, when I'd called that night in desperation, didn't really ask me if I wanted to go. She told me she was going to come pick me up. And then she didn't let me make no excuse. I had tried, of course, with my friend Angela coming by that day and needing to spend time with her and all. Shirley hadn't let that fly.

When I hung up the phone from talking to Mrs. Mary, after telling her, "All right. I'll check on you Wednesday night then," it dawned on me that if Shirley had given me more of a choice, I would likely be in jail, like Danny, or dead. I probably would have gone back, or I would have ended up killing Jim that one day and nobody would have been there to stop me. But I was following Shirley's directions concerning Mrs. Mary. I was doing my part. It wasn't up to me, I kept repeating to myself. It just may be that we all need a different approach to getting us where we need to be.

I walked into the kitchen and wrapped my arms around my mama.

Her back was to me as she was standing at the sink rinsing a fill-the-palm-of-your-hand ripe tomato. Hugging wasn't our usual M.O., but I went along with the good feeling I had inside. She kept to her washing, picking up a couple of pulled carrots. "Put some water on the stove to boil, now, Charlene. We need to brew some tea." I did.

32

More writing. Endless at times. I had to search deeper and write about all my garbage, put it out there for God—and Shirley—to see. I believed what my brother was doing was make believe. I had to write for pages my pain and the sickness of my anger. I had to then turn around and see my part in all of it. Shirley said it was the only way to be free. All the ladies that stuck around in my Thursday meeting had done it.

I could talk about all my suffering, and Lord knows I had. But until I was willing to dig my fingers into the dirt of the scared girl I was, afraid and blaming everybody else, I would stay helpless.

I didn't know for a right second how someone like Dakota was managing, hauling by herself her own misery. She had her apartment to focus on for the moment. She had new things. I was just beginning to let go of my old ideas.

I didn't want to go back to the woman I had been. I couldn't stand the thought of hating myself for the rest of my days. I wouldn't make it. I would wind up one big crazy, never to return. I believed that.

What I wanted was that "yeehaw" feeling I'd had in my Wild Woman dream in the hospital when she'd breathed air back into me, and I had gotten up and run out of the cave free. I wanted that feeling to stick tight.

§

The Wild Woman had been coming back to me, though not in dreams

189

like I'd hoped. I was sketching her like I was a wild woman myself, driven. I couldn't not draw her some days. I'd get up before my alarm on days I had to work to get time with her through my charcoals. I think it was healthy. It rooted me, firm within my own skin when I'd make that time.

I was working on getting the shading right and had been learning more about light and shadows from Tuesday night's art class. "It's called chiaroscuro shading, Charlie," Benjamin, the kind-faced man, had told me. He had come over to my bench one of the nights, saying he himself was only feeling so-so inspired to draw anything. He stopped behind me and watched for a while, then quietly asked what I knew about seeing the light.

Across the room, Older Burns said he tried not to "see the light" whenever possible because at his age you never knew if that was your maker calling you home. Chuckles broke around the room and Ned called out an "Amen" because he and Old Burns were close in age.

Benjamin was serious, though, and kept working with me over a couple of Tuesday evenings. He'd asked if I minded, of course, because that was the kind of man he was.

Nobody in the group was bothered by him giving me direction because his voice was quiet and soothing. I think, too, the others borrowed some of what he was telling me to use themselves. "We're all here to learn from each other," Older Burns would say, never failing to comment.

"That O.B., such a kind old fella, donating his spare change whenever he can." Younger Burns said, teasing Older Burns as if they were part of a stage show from one of them black-and-white goofy old TV shows. I'd gotten to see one or two of them in my AMC trailer TV-watching days and at the time thought they were nonsense. I thought anybody watching in those early days must have had the humor of a four-year-old. They would show the audience and all of them would be cracking the hell up over something somebody said that would have had Jim slapping me on the back of the head for opening my mouth with that kind of baloney.

Being around the two of them over a month or so, well, it was contagious.

Their playing around with each other was still corny as all get out but they had us all laughing. I guess everybody in our group, besides me and Dylan and Ginger, was over fifty, far as I could tell. And yet, there was hardly a difference—I started to see us all as kids. Big, unruly kids.

§

"You've got yourself a talent there, Charlie," Benjamin said to me that night as we were putting away our supplies. I heard him and looked up to see who else had heard. I caught Dylan's eyes. He just smiled. I didn't smile back. I looked at Benjamin like he was mad.

"You don't know it, but you do," he continued.

I said, "Okay. Thanks."

"Have you thought of applying to art school?" Thank God his voice was low and everybody else was blabbing away about one thing or the other. Ned was humming a song, and Mrs. Gillian said, "Oh, I love Cat Stevens."

"Charlie, you should consider it. It's not necessary but one day you could be a great artist." At that I smiled at him, doubtful. That was beyond anything I could imagine for myself. He might as well have said, "Charlie, have you thought about running for President?" I wanted to tell him that I didn't even have my diploma from high school. I was trailer trash. I didn't belong in college.

I looked down at my fingers, covered in charcoal. "Thanks, Benjamin. I have to think about it." That's all I could say. I needed to wash my hands and get some air.

On the way out, as Dylan was walking me to my car, he asked about what Benjamin had said. "You looked like you swallowed vinegar as he was talking to you."

"Oh, he said I might be talented—art school. He mentioned art school." Dylan stopped right in the middle of the street.

"What?" I said turning to look at him, a streetlight behind his head making it hard for me to see his face.

"I like it."

"You like what?"

"I agree with him," he said as if all he was saying was, "Sure, you should grab gum while you're in 7-Eleven getting some Doritos anyway."

"Dylan," I said, trembling, "You don't know me. I never finished high school. I dropped out to get married. I mean I'm not anymore, but that's what I did. I don't even have my GED."

"Well, get one," he said easy-peasy, no flinching. I was beginning to think I didn't like art night anymore. I didn't want to be around these people and their brainsick ideas for me. I was a waitress in a small mountain town. I wasn't no artist. I wasn't no college chick. I'd had a weird vision of a wolf-like, cave woman and couldn't seem to shake her. I liked to draw was all.

I had a hard enough time agreeing with Dakota to go to the creek at the college grounds to put my dang feet in the water. And if miracles of miracles were to take place, I couldn't imagine being twenty-three years old and being in classes with spoiled eighteen-year-olds who didn't know diddly about life and never had to question if they were worth something.

33

Time went by, as it does, and I was still mad at Danny thinking his redemption was made up. But the moment Benjamin had suggested I apply to art school and then Dylan had acted like it was no big deal for me to get my GED, I got an itching need to talk to my brother.

Danny had been writing me and Mama every other week or so since we saw him last. He sent Mama verses from the Bible that he liked and that helped him make it through his hard times, which I knew because she'd tell me. She'd be right near gleeful about it. "Blessed be, Charlene. Blessed be."

§

Mama was in her room reading the Bible like she did every night before going to sleep. I went to my room and pulled open my sock drawer where I'd stashed Danny's letters. I dumped them on the bed, then went through one by one and read them.

He had written me some of that religious hoo ha, too, but my letters had more of the scary real-real that happens when people are locked up, like how racism is even worse and how the white boys get it from the blacks, too. He wrote that you can't trust nobody and how the guards don't care if somebody fucks you up, so you better not count on them to protect you. He admitted to being nervous about having added that in the letter, since the guards might read it. I thought of the bee-stung-looking faced one.

Danny said a few things about his cellmate, the Frank he'd told Mama and me about when we visited. Frank Mason (Frank, because nobody dared to call him his given name of "Francis"), was in for the same reason as Danny, my guess was robbing a convenience store at gunpoint. In the letter, he explained that he couldn't give details to anything in case they'd confiscate them and use them as evidence against them when they're awaiting sentencing.

I wondered how many men were in for murdering their wives. I didn't even know if the law cared enough, like that night the officers came by after Candy's husband dragged her out of our meeting. Shirley had said that murder is murder but some men get away with it, like O.J. Simpson. I get mad if I think about it too much, it's so unfair.

Danny said that Frank was a blessing in disguise because even though he was black and three times the size of my brother, he was also clean and sober and into the Good Word. He said that he was safe because Frank had a reputation, though he couldn't say why. Maybe Frank had killed somebody. Danny said there's all kinds of drugs running in County and would be in prison, almost more so than on the outside. And that men are doing things to other men that they usually only do to women, which he said was the worst. He said that Frank claimed him as his bitch, so nobody could touch him. He said that other guys weren't so lucky.

I felt sick and had to put down the letter I was reading. Danny never called it "rape," but I knew that's what he meant. I hoped the men getting raped were the men that had been right evil to somebody else, like a story I'd heard about a husband raping his wife all night long at gunpoint. I could wish that on that kind of man.

I took out my notebook and tore out some pages and grabbed my pen to write him back. Reading his letters over, well, my being mad at him seemed to have come loose like a worn bandage. When I looked for reasons in my heart, holding the pen above the paper, they weren't there. I needed the one person who really knew me, the one who came from where I came from to know what stories were being sold to me.

I wrote him about Mrs. Gillian's art class at her house and the Wild Woman drawings I was doing. I told him about what Benjamin had said about me going to school for it and how far removed I was from reality to even think about it since I didn't have a goddamn GED, which none of them seem to think mattered.

I finished by saying that he'd looked pretty good the last time and that I was glad to see he was putting on weight. I didn't tell him that he had looked like Satan's bitch before, the thought making me laugh since now he claiming he was Frank's. I wrote him that I was glad Frank was around. I went to my sketch pad and found one of the smaller Wild Woman drawings I'd done, a quarter the size of a regular piece of paper, and tore it out. I took another piece and covered it before folding it carefully and tucking it in with the letter. I mailed it the next day. Mama was happy eyeing the address.

§

Thursday early, I called down to the Safe Depot to talk to Mrs. Mary about going to the meeting that night.

"Hi, Charlie." It was Lenore who answered. I was surprised she wasn't at the restaurant. "Mary's still here. One sec."

Mrs. Mary got on the phone, and I asked if she still wanted to go with me. She said she did, so I told her I'd pick her up at four, since the meeting started at five, but I liked to get there early. I was involved in all the setting up, getting chairs out and placed in a circle. I helped out with the meeting, so I could "stay in the middle." It was a saying the women had.

"I'll be here," Mrs. Mary said, her voice sounding low, disappointed about that fact. I understood.

I got off the phone and headed to the restaurant to work my lunch shift. Dakota was there. I told her about the idea for me to go to art school as she was heading into the cooler. "Sometimes the craziest things are the most likely to happen!" she shouted at me from inside before coming out, pushing the heavy door shut and laughing. "Hell, who would've thought I would have my own place!"

"I guess," I replied, not seeing how the two were related. I picked up an order sitting under the heat lamps ready to go out to my remaining table, not getting anymore flak from the cooks. As I walked out to the dining room, Dylan was standing near the bar, chatting it up with another fella I'd never seen before. Dylan looked over at me and smiled, eyes kind as usual.

I delivered the melted ham and cheese sandwiches to my table across the room and refilled their teas before going over to say hi. Dakota followed me, and I introduced her to Dylan and Dylan introduced us to his friend. Said his name was Paul and was originally from Tennessee and had only been in town for a month. "I work with this loaf," Paul said nudging Dylan.

Paul was shorter than Dylan with hair the color of red dirt clay. I couldn't figure why there was so many redheads in my life all of a sudden. He had tons of freckles and was semi-good looking, with a tight jaw and a dimple in his chin. I wasn't into stocky but Dakota lit up like someone hit the light switch. "Nice meeting you," she said almost in song, girly as I'd ever heard her, before turning to go tend to her last table of the day, an old couple that came in every Thursday and stayed the entire lunch time.

"I'd better get back to finishing up," I said. "Ya'll need anything?"

"We're good, Charlene Louise. But thank you. Can I call you later?" Dylan asked.

"Yes," I said, flushed from the day and from seeing him unexpectedly.

"Nice meeting you," Paul called out to me. There's two of them, I thought. Two men with manners, decent. It wasn't a movie like I had imagined but seemed so much better to me because it was real.

§

"Who-wee!" Dakota said later, us standing outside smoking before going back in to sweep and mop. "That was a fine man." I gave her a look. "Paul. He was fine," she said. "I mean, your man is cute, too, but I ain't looking at him."

"Good thing," I said mostly joking.

On my way over to pick up Mrs. Mary from the Safe Depot, I thought back to when Shirley first came to get me. I remembered her flute music and brown glasses that are now as comforting to me as clouds in the sky and water in a pond. I reminded myself that I wasn't there to save or convert Mary. I was doing as I had been told. I was getting good at taking directions. Seemed easier in the long run.

I had not thought about what we would actually talk about on the ride to the church. Would she prefer music and no talking? I didn't know what Mrs. Mary liked to listen to. I doubted it was Guns n' Roses or Metallica or Allman Brothers or Lynard Skynard. I had no idea. I wouldn't even know on the radio where to turn the dial, as I had never listened to anything that wasn't rock, Southern rock or country.

There was a part of town where most of the blacks lived, down by the electric company, and I'd had no reason to go down there. I'd never spent any time with a black person, neither, except passing by their kids in the halls in school or while shopping at the Ingles or Kmart.

Mrs. Mary was outside Safe Depot having herself a smoke when I drove up. I got a better look at her. Her eye seemed to be healing up all right. I had to go inside to let the girl answering the phones know I was the one taking Mrs. Mary off, as if I was responsible for her. I didn't like that too much. I thought she could do whatever the hell she wanted to. Since she had been at the house for a week, it was likely she'd made her decision to not go back to her husband. I told myself to rest assured she wasn't going to get any hair-brained ideas in the car with me.

Once on the road, she stared straight ahead like my mama had on the way to County jail. I wanted to explain to her that we were going to the opposite kind of place, a place where we got freedom.

"I was scared, too, when Shirley picked me up and took me to the church," I began. "You'll meet her. She's great."

"I don't need to go to no church," she said.

"Oh, well, this is different. This isn't church-church. I was confused about that, too. It's just a group that meets there."

She hmphed. "I ain't confused."

I kept going. "The ladies are nice. At first, I thought they were full of shit. One woman, you'll meet her, Willow, smiles a lot. But she's got one hell of a story and so it's good seein' her smile now." I was like a dribbling spigot, trying to convince Mrs. Mary there was nothing to worry about, until we pulled up to the back of the church, the sound of the gravel under my tires wrapping up my ramble, telling us we had now arrived.

The sun sat still in the sky. It was spring and the days were hanging on. I liked the way the air smelled coming in the rolled-down windows. "That's Carolina jasmine," Mrs. Mary answered the question I hadn't asked. "That sweet smell."

Nobody else was there yet. We got out of the car to smoke. Mrs. Mary pulled a can of Pepsi out of her purse and lit up a Salem 100. I had my remaining sweet tea from work that was mostly water from the melted ice cubes and lit my Marlboro Light. Her nails were painted a dark purple, almost a night color. She had long dark fingers and a simple gold ring with a tiny diamond on her left ring finger. That was her only jewelry. She wore blue jeans and a plain maroon-colored sweatshirt. I was at least a foot and a half taller than she was and stood like a giant across from her.

"How old are you?" she said out of the blue. It was the first time she looked directly at me and that lasted a second.

"Just turned twenty-three. You?" I went on, as she'd asked first anyway.

"Forty-five. Birthday's this June." She blew out a trail of smoke and then inhaled it back in as if doing a magic trick. "You ain't nothin' but a baby." I remember Jim's Daddy would inhale and never exhale. The smoke would come out as he'd be talking, like he was a demon.

She started up, "I been married to my husband since I was seventeen. I'd knowed him since we was younguns. Ne'er been away from 'im 'til now 'cept when he was on a run." As she talked, I saw how white her teeth were. I bet she had a beautiful smile, if ever she did. Her eyes were button brown and sharp as if she saw everything with them.

She took a hit on her cigarette, then looked at me like it was now my turn. In that moment, I wondered if the Wild Woman had visited her, too. But I didn't think a story about a hairy woman in a cave would be something she'd be wanting to hear if she hadn't.

"I married my husband when I was seventeen, too. Met him in high school though he was older." Then I thought of Jim dying and how I was grateful to not have known then, when I was getting away from him, that's what was going to happen to him and me. Who knew what was ahead of Mrs. Mary?

Just then Willow pulled up and Shirley right behind her. Next to Willow, in her front seat, sat straight and tall a man. What was she doing with a man? When he got out of the car and made his way over, I could see he had on eye liner. His hair was ash blond and was brushed neatly to his shoulders. His hips and hands swayed by his side. He walked like a woman! Willow was chatting in her usual way, as if he was.

"Hello!" she called out, her hand raised out to us, waving. "Let me introduce you. This here's Freedom." He stopped a foot short of Mrs. Mary, stuck his hand out, showing a couple of his fingernails painted near the same color as hers, who didn't seem to like that fact or him for that matter. Shirley had walked up, the smell of lavender easing off of her. I said hello to Freedom and so did Shirley, but Mrs. Mary turned and coughed the other way.

"This is Mary," I replied copying Willow. Freedom shifted his hips and with a bent wrist, flicked his hair off his shoulder.

Willow, cheerfully, seemingly unfazed by the weirdness between Freedom and Mary, asked him to follow her in to get the place set up. "We can help," I said eagerly. Mrs. Mary lit another cigarette and looked out to the parking lot as if she was not interested in helping and instead giving thought to her best route out.

I looked to Shirley. "Why's he helping her set up?" He did seem nice and all, but what the hell he was doing with Willow and what was he going to do while we were having the meeting in less than fifteen minutes?

"Because he's one of us, dear," she answered, calmly as usual. Mary hmphed again.

"But he's a man," I said, worried.

"It can happen to men, too, hon." I wasn't seeing how that was possible. Then I got to thinking about my brother in prison with all those other men and how he'd said that men will fuck other men and how he's safe only because he's Frank's pretend bitch.

"But...ain't he gay?" It made me nervous, the idea that he might talk in our meeting about what he did with other men. Reading the mention of it in my brother's letters was enough. And then I thought about how gay men started the whole AIDS thing. That had been the talk from the men around the tire shop, if the gay subject came up. Should I go in and wash my hands? Maybe Mrs. Mary knew and that's why she didn't shake his hand to begin with.

Shirley didn't seem too interested in making me feel better. "We all deserve to be here," she said before heading inside. With Shirley being the most loving person I knew, I felt ashamed of myself, even though I couldn't say why. I stayed standing still a moment, the day's sun fading and the air a light breeze on us, realizing I might have to rethink believing anything said at the tire shop and rethink my piss poor thoughts about someone like Freedom.

Each chair had a person sitting in it. As the shares went around the circle, Mrs. Mary chose to pass. I'd been checking on her the whole time as she'd taken a seat across from me, beside Elizabeth Ann. I caught her nod a couple of times as Elizabeth Ann shared. She'd changed a lot, wasn't as scared as she was in the early days. Her clothes were still crisp, neatly pressed. I avoided sitting next to her, as she made me feel like a slob.

Because of the two new people, the others felt more like talking about what it had been like, the wretchedness of our experience. We didn't hang in the past most of the time. We stuck to more positive conversations like being grateful for today and being relieved of our obsessions. Shirley once told me it was a way of helping the new folks relate so they'd stay. "It's how you build trust. Being vulnerable, too," she'd said.

When it was Freedom's turn to speak, he did. I admit I was curious as all get out to hear what this fruity man had to say about his situation. First, he thanked Willow for bringing him. He had a harder time, he felt, because there wasn't a safe house for him since he was a man. A couple of the women nodded in agreement. But not me or Mrs. Mary. She seemed to fidget more in her seat when he was talking.

He was staying at his sister's house, who was the only one in his family to still talk to him. But he said he'd met this handsome, wealthy fellow about a year before who he fell madly in love with. He couldn't say who it was, but the man had lots of money and a two-story house with columns (the house had columns!) and took care of his every need: food, clothes, a car. He said it was bliss for about six months and then things changed. The timer beeped and Willow interrupted gently, thanking him saying it was time to move on to the next person. He made a puny attempt to smile, ran his fingers through his hair and turned in the direction of the next person.

My story was not like his in many ways. I was jealous, too, that he'd met someone rich and that he'd had six months of what he called bliss. I didn't have none of that. Jim was an asshole from the beginning. We were dirt poor no matter that his family had that tire business. Jim drank away most of our money, and I'd always thought Jim's mama stashed bags of it under her mattress, where she kept herself most of her days, or else buried in their backyard. The Wilsons weren't bank folks.

Rich or poor, it didn't matter. Shirley and I had talked about it plenty as to why I was in love with Jim like I was. If he'd been charming and not an asshole, I probably wouldn't have thought twice about him. If he'd really paid me attention like I fantasized about, he wouldn't have registered. Shirley even said at one time that if he'd been decent, I probably would've thought he was ugly. Now, that's something. I tried to imagine him seeming ugly to me and couldn't get close.

Going back to thinking about Jim sometimes made me feel like something must have been terribly wrong with me to be with a man like that. I could go there quickly when I thought too much about me ever being with Jim. When I think to how I needed to be with him, it made me sick.

Shirley said that my past is an asset. Now that I'm not in danger, it's a positive thing I have. I had a hard time believing her until I met Mrs. Mary. The only reason why she even considered getting in the car with me is because she knew in some ways I'd been through what she'd been through. I know. It's not just words coming out of my mouth. I got it in my bones. My blood has pumped fear the same as her, for the same reason. My mind has told me the same lies. I know. She trusts me.

A few of the ladies introduced themselves to Mrs. Mary at the end of the meeting. She stood stiff. Even though she was standing next to me, it was like she was a yard off. She seemed to be tolerating us. Mrs. Mary made her way outside, away from more, "glad you're heres."

Willow stopped me as I was following her out and said, "You did good bringing her here, Charlie. We don't know yet what all she's been through. Probably scared to death, poor thing." She patted me softly on the arm. "One other thing," she added, "Don't push her to tell you anything. Let her in her own time."

"I will," I replied.

I understood Willow's advice, but the patience it required wasn't my favorite. Mrs. Mary didn't say anything the whole way back to the Safe Depot. When I put the car in park, she got out first, quick as if we had been on some awkward date and she didn't want me making a move on her. I had to go in to let them know it had been me to drop her off. Before walking up the stairs toward her room, she turned and said she wanted to go again. "Next week then?" I asked, surprised.

She said, "Yes." I told her I'd call her like the last time and waved goodnight.

35

The weather was getting warmer and Dakota was still nagging me about heading down to the college to walk after work. "I'm bored with being inside all the damn time," she said, flying past me, hands balancing stacked glasses and used silverware making her way back to the dishwasher. Tourist season was picking up and so was the lunch rush.

"I don't think I got the energy for it, girl," I said to her. "My feet hurt as it is."

"That's why we'll go stand in the creek after. The water's cold enough. It'll be good for the circulation." She was getting stubborn about it, as I had been making excuses for weeks. Either it looked like it was going to rain, I was too tired, or Mama needed help or a meeting. But that afternoon, I had no plans and the weather was sixty-five degrees and blue skies.

"All right, Dakota," I said. "It can't hurt to go for a walk." She let out a hoot.

§

Dakota drove us down to the college on the backside of the school, near the small gym. People from town parked there all the time, she told me, as if it were okay for us to do the same. I only halfway believed her. Dakota did whatever she wanted whenever she felt like it. I had the unfunny feeling a group of college kids were going to stampede from over the grassy hill in front of us, shouting, "No white trash allowed!" Dakota put the car in park and hopped out. I followed her, as she made her way along the edge of the gravel road to the creek that ran through the middle of campus.

There were trees that lined the creek. A slight breeze blew that tinkered with the new leaves dangling from the branches.

"Ain't these river birch somethin'!" Dakota shouted. I hoped she wasn't going to be yelling out at every blade of grass she liked along our walk, drawing more attention to us, though she was right. It was something mighty pretty to be looking at.

The campus had pink flowering dogwood trees in bloom, too. "Them's Jesus trees," I told Dakota. "That's what they used to hang Jesus." My mama loved this time of year, because she felt that Jesus was all around, blooming his resurrected heart out. When I told Dakota, she buckled over, hands on both knees getting a good laugh in.

Through gasps of air she managed, "Oh Lord, Charlie, your mama does sound like my Aunt Rosaline. Did I never tell you about her?"

"Day one, I believe."

Dakota straightened herself back up, slapped her hands together. "Well, then you know." We were walking for what felt like miles, making our way around a field where an empty running track sat in the middle. There were mountain tops off in the distance on one side and then the other. We were walking at a clip. I started sweating bullets, the collar of my work shirt sticking to my neck.

Dakota started skipping ahead of me. That girl seemed to have more energy than a flea party on a dog's belly. I was about ready for a cigarette myself. Must have been twenty minutes already, and my throat was parched up. We weren't creek side anymore, or I'd have stuck my face in it for a sip.

Our walk had been a huge circle, where we wound up back near the gym where we'd parked. "Doors open. Gotta pee," Dakota said at the side entrance, like we were allowed to walk in, as if we were heading to basketball practice.

"I ain't goin' in there," I said to her, ready to take my thirsty ass to the gas station for a Pepsi or see if the ice had melted from my tea in the car. I'd make do.

"Nobody's gonna say nothin', Charlie," she said, disappearing inside, beyond the heavy metal and glass doors. I wished I had some of her not caring so much what other people thought, but the idea of getting told I don't belong some place made me think I'd rather not take my chances. "Come on," she said, sticking her head back out, roll-waving her arm at me. I shook my head and turned around. I cut my way through the grass, toward the parking lot.

She ran up behind me. Next thing, Dakota pointed across the way to a large building with a weird metal sculpture out front that looked like it belonged in a scrap yard. "Let's head over there."

"What for?"

"That's the art building." I could feel the blood rush up my ears and could hear my heart as if somebody was knocking a knuckle on my chest.

"Why is it I need to go there?" I asked. I wanted to say, "Back off, Dakota," but knew it wouldn't do any good. My stubborn would never beat out hers.

"Because, girl, you're gonna go there. You might as well get used to it." She took my arm and pretended to full-body drag me across the parking lot. Half of me could have passed out but half secretly wanted to see what it was like inside an art building. I wouldn't admit that to anyone.

There were both guys and girls going in and out the front. They did look so much younger than me. They looked like real grunge, the natural kind, while I was the worn, tired, local redneck kind. They carried these big black folders with handles. I'd seen them at Mrs. Gillian's store. I'd thought about getting one for my drawings, as I just stuffed my papers in my drawing pad or rolled them up.

Dakota marched right through the doors like she went to art school every day. I went in behind her, looking only at the tile in front of my feet. The air smelled like a mixture of metal shop, paint and chalk. She stopped suddenly, and I about knocked her over. She was reading a sign that had room numbers and names listed. "What are you looking for?" I asked. Did I really want to know?

"I thought we could find the office."

"Dakota. I ain't goin' into no office to talk to nobody..." And just before I could finish, she told me to come on because we were two doors away. I followed her. It was all I could do.

There was a clock on the wall behind the lady at the front desk that looked like the ones in high school. All schools must have the same clocks. It was 4:30. There was a name tag on the counter that said Geraldine Fletcher, Administrative Assistant. Mrs. Fletcher looked busy, sorting papers in brown folders, but Dakota spoke up.

"Excuse me," she said to Mrs. Fletcher, who kept her eye on her sorting, only nodding her head. "Say a person is interested in going to school, for art. What does that person need to do?" I couldn't tell if the sweat on my back was from our walk or new. My nerves were heating me up.

Mrs. Fletcher looked up at us standing there. She seemed to look us over. Dakota was giving her the usual gap-tooth grin, wearing an XL sized t-shirt, nearly swallowing her whole. Then she looked at me in my shirt with the name, Lenore's, sewed into it.

I thought this Mrs. Fletcher was going to tell us to stop wasting her time. I thought she was going tell us to stop wasting our time.

"Well, now I'm Mrs. Geraldine Fletcher and you are?" Dakota said her name first. I mumbled out something close to Charlene Louise, and Dakota butted in, "This here's Charlie." Dakota's smile nearly passed the edges of her face when Mrs. Fletcher asked me if I worked for Lenore.

"I do," I managed, feeling hotter and sweatier than two minutes prior, noticing how dry my throat was, even more so after the long walk, no water, and shame rising up for us being there.

Mrs. Fletcher told us she knew Lenore real well. She smiled at me. "She's a good person to work for," she said. Dakota and I nodded together.

Mrs. Fletcher got up from behind her desk and came out to where we were standing. She had on a long, black skirt and dark, black tights and black shoes that later Dakota told me were Mary Janes. She passed us over to a bookshelf that had trays in it. "Here you go," she said handing Dakota a packet of paper. "This is what you'll need to know. I'm assuming, but could be wrong, that you're not enrolled with the college yet?"

I didn't know how Dakota did it, but she didn't blink or twitch or stumble. She just said, "Nope," as if it was every day that all art students were two redneck girls with no education. "Could we get two?" Dakota asked, looking at me who'd had my head glued to that metal clock on the wall. It was five past when we had walked in. Time was moving as slow as a river full of mud.

Mrs. Fletcher handed me the other packet. "Nice to meet you girls. Stop by any time if you have questions. I'll be happy to help." She reached out to shake our hands. Dakota thanked her for us, and I tried to smile while holding the packet of papers in my hand as if it was a map to a hidden treasure I wasn't so sure I was ready to find.

"You look like shit," Dakota said as we went outside.

"I need a smoke."

"Kinda pale, like me, which doesn't seem right," she said.

"Some things are easier for you," I said.

"Maybe," Dakota said. "But you always do what you need to do. You're a badass at heart."

We stood in the parking lot and chain-smoked, talking about everything but art and school. We talked so long, I had to pee something furious. There was no way I was going back in one of them buildings, so I told her it was time I got on home.

§

"You got a letter from Danny," Mama called out to me from the kitchen when she heard me get in.

"Thanks, Mama!" I yelled back in her direction. "I see it," I replied, shaky with nerves to see he'd written me back. I couldn't wait to read it, but instead put it in my room on my bedside table until before going to bed.

"What's for dinner?" I asked, walking in the kitchen. Mama had the ironing board set up on the other side of the table near the back door. She had her religious radio on in the background. She used the same iron, heavy, that she'd used forever. Steam blew as she ran it over the quilt she had just finished.

Without looking up at me, she told me that I could fix a sandwich or something and that she'd not gotten around to making anything. It was rare that she didn't cook, and since I'd been living there, I'd eaten better than I had in years living in the trailer with Jim.

"Aren't you gonna eat?" I asked her. She nodded, still fully concentrating on her ironing. "All right. I'll make us both a sandwich then." I wanted to talk about the college but thought better of it. She seemed pleasantly occupied, and I couldn't handle the kinds of questions I didn't have the answers for.

I made us pimento cheese sandwiches with some chips and sweet pickles. She folded the quilt with so much care she might as well have been folding the American flag. I offered to help but she wouldn't let me. She and my new buddy, Dakota—the two as stubborn as a breech birth.

We ate without saying too much. She talked a little about some of the local gossip from church, whose cooking had gone downhill for Wednesday night suppers and who had been sick recently. I hadn't been with her to service in some time, which I was hoping she wouldn't bring up. I sat there grateful that other people's shortcomings were more interesting to her than the purity of my soul that night. Mine was needing a break.

§

"Been a long day, Mama. Gonna turn in for the night." I was ready to get to bed early, mostly so I could read my letter, to have time with it.

"Don't forget your prayers, Charlene. Sleep tight."

I snuggled in under the covers and slowly opened the letter. My brother's handwriting was tiny and neat, as if he'd been some kind of honor student. He was also a good speller, which I wasn't.

The letter was two notebook pages long and half was about him and half was about me. He wrote how excited he was to have gotten my letter and even more excited to get my drawing. He said that he was proud of his little sister, because I had real talent and had to do something with it. "Don't let it go to waste, Charlie. I won't let you," he wrote. The last of his letter, he wrote that if I worked on getting my GED, then he would, too. From prison.

I held the letter and put my face in my pillow and cried and cried, but I wasn't sad. I had never been happier.

RESOURCES

While this book is fiction, the issues addressed are real (domestic violence and addiction). If you or someone you know is suffering, please seek help. The first step in healing is to ask for help, to not do it alone.

You. Are. Worth. It.

National Domestic Violence Hotline
thehotline.org

Alcoholics Anonymous (AA)
aa.org

Narcotics Anonymous (NA)
na.org

Al-Anon Family Groups (Al-Anon)
alanon.org

National Institute of Mental Health (NIMH)
nimh.nih.gov

**This book is not affiliated with any of the above organizations. This is a list the author put together and wanted to make available to her readers.

ABOUT THE AUTHOR

RACHEL MARGARET DREWS is a teacher, an artist and the author of her debut novel, Wild Woman. She is originally from Clemson, SC (a big Clemson Tiger fan). She lived in Los Angeles for 11 years primarily working in visual effects for feature films and commercials. Rachel has been a part of two Oscar-winning VFX teams! In 2018 she moved back to Brevard, NC, where she lives amongst the landscape she writes about in her work. Visit her website at racheldrews.com, and follow her on Instagram @rachelmdrews for more information about all of the above and to stay connected!